THE KEEPER OF LIGHT

A.J. NORA

I0777790

Lion Briar
Books
INDEPENDENT PUBLISHING

LION BRIAR BOOKS LLC

Paperback: 978-1-967056-04-0

Ebook: 978-1-967056-02-6

Lion Briar Publishing

ajnorabooks.com

Author's Note

This novella is available in ebook on my newsletter list. If you'd like to get the ebook for free, visit my website ajnorabooks.com.

This is a no spice queer epic fantasy with romance. If you'd like content warnings, please head to my website (https://ajnorabooks.com/content-warnings-for-kingdoms-of-kaelums/to get the full list.)

For my husband, who taught me that true love is worth the effort.

Pronunciation Guide

Silvis: SIL-vis

Brynia: BRI-nee- yah

Anastasia Behar: An-NUH-stay-zuh Bay-HAR

Meredith Kaesy: Mare-UH-dith KAY-see

Alixandra Bludeg: Al-ix-AN-dra BLU-deg

Creon: KREE-on

Vasileios Maeb-Somni: Va-ssee'-lee-os Mahb-SOM-nee

Shiloh Leigdraca: SHY-low Lē(d)zh-DRA-ca

THE SOMNIUM SEA
DREAMER RIVER
SINK FALLS
KAESY
KHENT
DAES RIVER
SHEEPSGROVE FOREST
SILVER MOUNTAINS
THE ABYSSAL BAY
HOLLOW DESERT
UVIEL
THE CAPITAL
QUEEN'S CREEK
CAINE
SILVIS
SEAI
MAJESTY MARSH
Nord

CHAPTER I

Meredith

In the desert above Haven, a horse-drawn carriage rattled along the narrow sandstone path. The darkness of night coated the landscape, but the barest touch of sun yawned at the horizon, signaling dawn would soon break fully on the Silvid Desert. Meredith, daughter of Duke Kaesy and honorary knight, stared out the tiny window, marveling at the stone path that cut through the dunes.

Meredith's eyes drifted from the pale sand to land on her mate, one of the queen's most decorated knights and daughter of General Xander. Alix wore leathers—her traveling armor, despite the short distance from the shore to the city of Haven. She kept her ashen blonde hair braided against her scalp, away from her face, and up into a ponytail that, with each bounce of the carriage, brushed against the edge of her pointed ears and sharp jawline—something that irritated Alix greatly. Despite the many times Meredith had suggested Alix cut her hair—short like Meredith's own hair, Alix had refused. She kept it long and braided like her father's—the beloved General Xander.

Alix turned her icy blue eyes to Meredith and the stern expression melted into a gentle adoration. "Enjoying the scenery, my love?" Alix's deep tones rattled in her chest and soothed something wild that fluttered in Meredith.

"The desert is ..." Meredith searched for words and twined her fingers with Alix's on the cushioned bench between them. The endless rolling sands, broken only by the sandstone roads created by the magic of ancient Silvid mages, glittered in the first rays of sunrise. "Beautiful," Meredith finally said, though the word did not encompass the landscape before her.

"Not nearly as beautiful as you," Alix said. A smirk tugged at her lips, tempting yet comforting. Meredith leaned over and stole a quick kiss—a mere brushing of lips. Alix's fingers tightened on Meredith's, and she chased her lips as Meredith pulled away, giving her a hard kiss that left Meredith feeling fizzy inside.

With a deep breath to settle her thoughts, Meredith said, "Don't you find it amazing that these roads were built by magic?" Her ancestors made this road with their magic, made the city she was travelling to, made all the temples of the Silvid Desert. And yet, despite the amazing feats of magic from many centuries past, the other nobles—and the queen herself—didn't see magic the way Meredith did. Even Alix despised Silvid magic, so Meredith wasn't surprised by Alix's response.

She scoffed. "Amazing? More like a nice side effect to a curse." Much like most Silvids, Alix thought their magic was perverse—a curse that brought nothing but misfortune on those who used it. It had been Silvid magic, after all, that had torn the continent apart, creating the two countries: Brynia and Silvis, which had once been a joined nation.

Meredith changed the subject, wishing her attempts to warm Alix to magic didn't all fail in the exact same way. "Are our contacts in Haven aware of our arrival?"

"Yes, of course, Mere." Alix sighed and turned her gaze to the desert beyond the window, just over Meredith's shoulder. "What did the reports say, again? Wolves?"

Meredith shook her head and her short black hair flopped against her cheeks. "Well, yes, but no. Were you not listening this morning?"

Alix winked. "I'm your blade. Point me, and there I will go."

Meredith sighed dramatically as amusement played in her eyes. Her loyal, beloved Alix. "Several reports described something wolf-like, but certainly not wolves—at least not anything natural, anyway."

"So, the Court of Bones interfering? Raising the dead?" Alix dipped her head and Meredith could almost see the thoughts running through her mind—all the enemies of Silvis, the motives, and means. "Possibly rebels," she muttered, "or a bid for power from one of the other courts."

"Much more interesting," Meredith said.

Alix's head jerked to attention, Meredith's words pulling her from her thoughts. "Mm?"

"I believe the creatures terrorizing the countryside are Hollows."

Alix scoffed and tapped her fingers against Meredith's hand, where their fingers still tangled together. "Ridiculousness, Mere. You're smarter than that. Hollows are a myth—a legend, an allegory, if anything, for what happens if you use magic."

Meredith removed her hand from Alix's. "I'm smart enough to have read *significantly* more than you. While you were out playing with the Knights, I was being trained to be a valuable asset to the prince. My mother actually cares about our family line, about the generations beyond us." Meredith crossed her arms and turned to the window.

"Do you really have to bring this up again?" Alix asked. She sighed and flopped back against the carriage seat. "At least my mother—commoner that she is, actually cares if I'm happy. She wouldn't sell me off to the highest bidder for—what? Generational wealth? Land?"

"Security. Ambition. I could be the queen, but I don't expect you to understand."

"Is that why you won't tell your mother that I'm your mate?"

"I have!" Meredith cried. "You don't think I've told her? I've tried to tell her. She doesn't believe me, but who would with the way we argue? With how weak the thread is between us." The bond thread humming in her chest was a golden, fragile, and fluttering thing. Her mother's insistence on marriage would surely snap the thread when it finally separated them. She couldn't handle that. If only she could find someone who would marry her on paper only, she could still be with Alix. Someone who wouldn't expect anything of her—not even an heir. An impossible dream. She didn't want to think about the impending pain awaiting her future, so she didn't.

Meredith stared out the window as the sun's first warm rays touched the sand. In the distance, a hulking shadow raced across the dunes.

"What ... was that?" Meredith asked, pointing out the window to where the creature pitched itself forward into the ground and disappeared. Alix leaned forward, following the line of Meredith's finger as the beast disappeared.

"Some desert creature returning to its den for the day? A fox, or a wolf, I suppose. I'm sure you know more about what lives in this desert than I do, considering your *significant* reading habit," Alix said, leaning back against her side of the carriage bench.

"No. Too big," Meredith said. Her voice dropped to barely a whisper. "That's the beast we're searching for, I'm certain of it. We should follow it."

"Into a hole in the ground? Absolutely not. This will be a *safe* investigation," Alix said, narrowing her eyes at Meredith.

The carriage turned sharply and the Western Temple suddenly came into view, seeming to rise from the dunes. The white stone gleamed in the first rays of dawn, nearly glowing against the still-dark sky. Ancient Silvids, with their magic able to shape the earth, clearly formed the temple from the sand. The pillars twisted in intricate ways. Stairs climbed up engraved sandstone blocks, leading to enormous doors carved and glowing with the golden magic of the Havenites. Meredith looked on in awe. *This* is the power of our magic, she thought.

The carriage stuttered to a stop and the memory of the beast disappearing into the desert slammed back into her mind. Meredith chewed on her lower lip. They were at Haven's doorstep now, which meant the beast was dangerously close to the city. They had to tell someone, do something. What if it was already too late?

CHAPTER 2

Anastasia

Blue mosslight filtered into Anastasia's bedroom from the underground city beyond her apartment. Her eyes cracked open as her body processed what had woken her—a pounding on the front door.

She glanced at the clockwork on the wall, its tiny wooden hands pointing out the time. It wasn't even dawn yet. Blood drained from her face. Was there an emergency? Was someone in trouble? She leapt out of bed, pulling a dagger from her bedside table, as she raced to the front door, which rattled on its hinges.

"Anastasia!" came a booming, and familiar, voice from the other-side of the door. Her father. Tension kept her taut as she removed the chain from the door. As soon as the chain fell away, the door opened. Anastasia had to jump back to stay clear of the heavy door swinging inwards.

She crossed her arms, tightening them against her chest, as the dagger's edge slid against her side, biting at the flesh with its cool sting. She'd forgotten the blade, but the pain helped clear her mind as she took in her father's stern expression.

Commander Creon, the leader of Haven, stood in the open doorway. He was an imposing man, banded with muscle formed from decades of training. His once-black hair, now kissed with streaks of gray, lay neat and pristine, where he had pushed it from his forehead and slicked it back. His golden eyes, bright like flickering flames, took in her uneasy stance with a frown.

"What is it, Father?" Anastasia said.

"You need to get dressed and come down to City Hall."

Her stomach dropped with dread. Her mind raced, imagining a hundred different scenarios. Haven was safe. As far as her history lessons told her, the city had been safe for centuries. "What do you mean? Has something happened? Is anyone hurt? Has there been some incident with the fae?"

"Calm yourself, child," Creon said, shaking his head in disapproval. "We are to have guests from the Court of Dreams. You will aid them in their investigation."

"Fae? The fae are coming to Haven? Why? What are they investigating? We have done nothing wrong." Cool air from the city beyond the open door whipped around, fluttering Anastasia's nightgown.

"The fae can explain when you meet with them. For now, make yourself presentable. You are the Keeper of Light—act like it. If you are ever to lead Haven, to take my place, then you cannot let your emotions get the better of you." He shook his head, muttering as he turned away. "Panicking like a child." His hand rested on the doorknob.

"Yes, Father," Anastasia said, despite the questions burning on her tongue, despite the emotions still churning in her stomach.

"Be at City Hall in no more than an hour," he said. He didn't even give her time to respond as he exited the tiny apartment, closing the door hard behind him.

Anastasia stared at the dark wooden door. Now, alone in the darkness of her apartment, she waved her hand and fire sparked, jumping from lantern to lantern until the room glowed with warm firelight. The light flickered, illuminating the sparseness of her home. Since moving out of her parents' home, which was unfortunately only a block or two down the street, she hadn't bothered decorating. Her apartment was just a place to sleep and store her things. No one ever came to visit her, except her father—and much like this time, his visits were usually unpleasant. Even Shiloh, her only friend, hadn't visited yet. For the last few years, he'd been completely immersed in mage training. He was adamant that he would become a court mage and stay at her side when she took Creon's role as commander.

Her father would probably chastise her if he were still here to see her use the ancient flame so irreverently, but she didn't care. She wasn't fond of the blue mosslight lanterns used by the entire underground city, where she, and all the other humans in the fae realm, lived. Homes were lit with bioluminescent blue. The streets were bathed in it. She was sick of blue. The warm orange and red of her flame chased away the mosslight.

Fire was a comfort she would never abandon, but Haven was beautiful in its own way. She moved to the window and peered out at the quiet city. She lived at the city center, only a short walk from City Hall and the plaza there, so the tall buildings and the narrow streets limited her view. From her window, all she could see was the building across the street—a proper apartment building. Her home was more of a town house—a perk of being the Keeper, she guessed. Her mind wandered as she imagined the familiar city beyond.

The city's cavern was immense; its ceiling resembled a star-filled night sky, punctuated by the glimmer of wild moss growing on the cave walls—the very moss the inhabitants used for their mosslights. A river split the cavern in half—on one side, the city sat and on the other a stretch of dark soil and the great stairs that led to Silvis and all the fae lands beyond.

Centuries ago, Haven was built entirely of the stone beneath it. She wished she could have seen its construction, but she had heard the stories of the magic of its creation. Silvid fae—mages of the elements—had used their magic to create enormous buildings, pulling the stone from the ground itself and forcing it into these tall box shapes. There was a beauty in the stone as the fae let the earth decide what to use. Some buildings were cool grey stone, others a twist of colors—sandstone, granite, marble. Alongside the fae, the human mages had used their magic flames to create glass panes, and, together, they installed windows—including a lot of stained-glass, which was a sacred art form of Haven.

A lost art form. Fewer humans were born with the ancient flame and somewhere along the line, knowledge of how to create the glass was lost.

The building just across from her only had a few stained-glass panes left, with most having to be fixed with an uncolored glass in recent years. The windows were all dark—too early for her neighbors to be up; she guessed. Despite the time, a few people wandered the streets. They laughed and talked as they made their way deeper into the city. Were those the guests her father had mentioned? She squinted her eyes and leaned against the window. No. The small group seemed all human. In fact, looking closer, she recognized them. Three of her father's favored knights—Marcus, Damien, and Sarah. She grimaced. What could possibly be going on?

Pulling herself away from the window and back to her room, she started getting ready. The sooner she got to City Hall, the sooner she could figure out why the fae were visiting Haven. She tossed her dagger onto the bed and ran fingers across her side where she'd felt the sting of the blade. No blood. She frowned. The dagger must be more dull than she'd realized to have only left a bloodless scratch. Time to sharpen it, she thought, as she moved around her room in silence to get ready for the day.

With her trousers and tunic hastily pulled on, she began braiding her long blonde hair away from her face. She stood in front of the mirror as she looped the braids into intricate patterns that hung like slack rope around her face and twisted down her back. Her armor glistened in the gentle light of her bedroom.

Every day, she wore her knight's garments, even though there hadn't been danger in Haven for centuries, as far as she knew, anyway. The armor was part of her duty as the Keeper of Light. She was the hero, the protector, even when there was no one to save. She hoped there would never be a need to save her people, but would gladly throw herself between them and any enemy that dared harm the Havenites.

Anastasia trained like the other knights did—every day as if war were on their doorstep. In some ways, she supposed her father was prudent in this. As a settlement of humans in a fae realm, they couldn't let their guard down, no matter how many centuries their ancestors had lived in the little city sanctuary of Haven.

After her hair was neatly in place, Anastasia pulled her armor from its stand with a loving tenderness she rarely showed, second only to her love of her sword. The sword, a longsword with gold glittering at the hilt and sigils of protection engraved along the blade, was a Keeper relic. She treasured it for the precious heirloom it was, while still remembering it was her weapon and a tool to be used. So, she kept it on a mount near the door—easy to access and practical, but still special. She didn't keep many weapons in her house, but always had a dagger by her bed. With the dagger in her bedroom and the sword on her way out the door, she was prepared for emergencies that had never come.

The armor was much like every other piece of Haven armor—mostly leather, lightened as much as possible, chainmail tasset and collar, all of which were enchanted with heat dispelling sigils by the mages of Haven. Though they rarely went up to the desert during the day, the sigils were a precaution that her father made sure were on each piece of new armor. The leather cuirass bore the emblem of Haven on the chest—a golden sun, with red lines around the edges, and a bright white sword plunging down through the center. The only thing that set her armor apart from the rest were a few extra sigils that she didn't know the purpose of, but they were elaborate and quite beautiful in red thread. Her father had told her once that the extra sigils were protective, providing a bit of an extra spark should she need it.

Her thoughts wandered to training. Would the guests keep her out all day? She didn't particularly like missing her daily routine, though she figured there would be no one to miss her. Her father had her train separately from most of the knights—she was special, he'd always say, she needed to work harder than the others.

Creon had always been hard with her training. Since the moment she could hold a sword, he'd had her in training, which only got worse when her magic manifested. When her magic had first started developing, the brief flickers of golden flame had amazed her. She'd obsessed over the newfound ability, but now it was just another shackle to her father's demands. Being one of the humans blessed with magic, she had to be trained for battle, especially since the Flame's Trial that Havenites all took as children marked her as the Keeper of Light—the chosen descendant of Haven's first flame. Anastasia always thought calling it the Flame's Trial made it sound much more ominous than it was in reality, since the trial consisted of patting a dragon statue on the nose to see if the glass orbs of its eyes lit with fire or not.

The statue was, Anastasia always assumed, a sort of magic channel or amplifier to help identify people born with the flame. When she'd touched it, fire had blasted around the dragon's eyes and dripped to the ground like tears. Shiloh's trial was also more explosive than most other children—though not quite as strong as hers—so he'd immediately gotten an invitation from the mages tower.

With Shiloh also caught in the machinations of Haven politics, Anastasia's life was incredibly lonely. He would be a court mage one day and they, along with the rest of Haven's council, would be responsible for the welfare of the people. A duty she was proud of, passionate about, even, but an empty ache plagued her and settled in her chest any time she saw the smiling faces of Haven or the camaraderie between the knights.

Anastasia sighed and pulled herself from her melancholy reverie. Her father was expecting her at City Hall. She wanted to keep him waiting, nearly crawled back into bed, but Anastasia wasn't that kind of girl.

Keepers were only born, she'd been told, once every century and possessed the power of the first fire mage of Haven— Flame. Her great, great grandfather had been the last Keeper. Almost always, Keepers came from the same bloodline, as if the sacred fire were being passed down through the generations.

Anastasia straightened her armor and pulled on the matching leather boots, which were steel-toed and wrapped in a strange, lace-like chainmail that held more heat-dispelling sigils in the metal's twist itself. In her Keeper's armor, she was a symbol of protection, and the responsibility leaders had for those beneath them. She may have a complicated relationship with her father, but she loved Haven and the people in it. Anastasia didn't don the armor because he told her to. She did it for them.

Anastasia took her sword from its mount and fastened it to her side before slipping out into the hallway and into the city beyond.

The street was quiet, empty, yet the air rippled with malice. Anastasia scanned the shadows of the surrounding buildings. Cold stone greeted her gaze and the chilly shimmer of blue mosslight glinted off of the glass. A shifting of the wind brought a stench, like rot, to her nose and she nearly gagged. At the corner of her vision, a hulking presence moved. She pulled her sword in an easy, swift movement, turning to the strange beast before her.

"Wha-" she said, fumbling for thoughts as the full sight of the creature came into view. It was a beast like she'd never seen before. It stood on four massive paws and stood nearly as tall as herself, which was impressive as she was a rather tall woman. Wolf-like, but not. It had a massive wolf's head with jaws that opened too far back, teeth in jagged rows that seemed unending. Its midnight flesh hung loose on its body, revealing flesh and bone dripping with sludgy black blood. Fur of shadow and smoke sparsely covered its hide. The look in its red eyes screamed of hunger, of pain. For a moment, she saw the beast as any other creature—alone, afraid, and perhaps hungry. A brief wave of pity washed through her that quickly turned to fear as the beast lunged towards her, snarling with fatal intentions.

Her blade clashed against its teeth as its heavy paws rained blows down on her chest, nearly knocking her to the ground. Pushing with all of her strength, she twisted and tossed the monster away from her. There was no one else around. She was alone. She couldn't take this thing by herself. What should she do? Scream? She was the Keeper. She couldn't yell out for help. Who would come save her?

Once again on its feet, the beast's gaze landed on her. What choice did she have but to fight? She focused on the golden pool of fiery magic in her soul, calling forth the ancient flame. As she stood her ground, staring down at the beast, fire exploded down the length of her sword. She wouldn't let this beast pass her without a fight. It was her duty to protect Haven, so she would.

CHAPTER 3

Anastasia

Anastasia lunged out of the way of the wolf-beast's snarling jaws. How long had she been fighting this creature? Her shoulders dipped with exhaustion. She needed to deal with it before the morning carriage and pedestrian traffic started pouring in. Few people were out before dawn, but fear pulsed in her veins, fueling the spurts of fiery magic that sizzled down her blade. She circled the beast, and it circled her in turn.

Its shadowy fur whipped around the length of its body, waving as if from some invisible wind. Red sparks of lightning that matched the haunting red glow of the creature's eyes, twisted around the lengths of its legs. She sliced her blade through the air, tossing a blade of fire towards the beast. Its eyes went wide, and it threw itself aside, desperately scrambling away from the flames. It stumbled back and then forward again, whining and snapping its jaws towards her.

Another wave of curious pity washed through her. Was the creature hurt? hungry? rabid somehow? Afraid of fire?

She shook her head. She couldn't risk letting it go, couldn't risk it getting away and harming the rest of Haven. Anastasia cast her eyes around the street. She'd never done it before, but perhaps she could make a wall of flame to trap the creature. That sort of magic usually required spells or other channels, but she wasn't practiced in using sigils or spell words.

In her moments of hesitation, the wolf-beast had circled closer until it slid behind her. Before she could angle herself away, it launched at her legs, latching onto her hip with jagged teeth, piercing through the chainmail as if it were paper. Blood gushed and scented the air with its coppery tang. Anastasia cried out at the sudden pain and twisted her sword in her hands until the blade pointed down towards the beast's head. With all the strength she could muster from her exhausted muscles, she drove the tip of the blade towards its eye.

It twisted its face at the last moment and her sword slid across its cheek, opening a deep gash. Black blood poured from the wound, dripping onto the ground as she continued her attack, burying her sword in the wolf-beast's shoulder. Its jaws tightened and shook, eliciting a scream from Anastasia's lips. Still screaming, she poured every ounce of flame that she could muster down her faithful sword.

Dancing flames ringed in ethereal golden light rushed down the blade and exploded into the beast's body, engulfing them both in a red-hot blaze. Once again, Anastasia was glad for her natural immunity to fire. The beast's weight pulled on her as life left its burnt body. She fell to her knees as the flames still danced across her skin and the corpse of the beast. She struggled for breath as the smoke and the stench of the creature rose to her nose.

She pushed it away, dislodging its fangs from her flesh with another pained yelp. Her blood mixed on the stone with the black blood of the beast. She stared at it with disgust, trying to decide what to do. She pressed her hand against her own wound. It was deep. She didn't think she'd be able to walk like this—and she was so tired, too tired to maintain her flames. She sank to the cold stone and closed her eyes.

The flames finally dissipated, but she could taste soot on her tongue and smell the ash lingering in her nostrils. The taste of soot alarmed her less than it should. It was one of the first signs that she was beginning to burn—that using magic was draining her soul and burning her from the inside out. No one had burned since she'd been alive, but as the Keeper, she was at a much higher risk. Her mother warned her constantly that overusing her magic was dangerous. As Keeper, her magic was volatile, powerful, and at times unpredictable.

Laying on the ground with that terrifying taste on her tongue, Anastasia realized an unfortunate truth—she'd used too much of her magic and she was bleeding far too much. Her eyes fluttered open as she forced herself into motion.

Putting weight on her uninjured hip, she slid across the stone, clawing across the ground towards the plaza. Someone would be there. There was a meeting. Had an hour gone by? Would her father come out to look for her?

"What the f-" said a strange woman's voice behind her. As she turned, two fae women with their luggage surprised her; they stood a few feet away from her and the dead wolf-beast. The woman who spoke wore a blonde ponytail, braided at her temples, and looked like a warrior—dressed in leathers and bound in muscle. The taller woman was lithe but seemed deadly in her grace. Her shrewd eyes took in the scene.

"Alix, go fetch the leader of this place! I'll tend to the girl," the graceful woman said. Relief and anxiety mingled in Anastasia's gut. She needed help, but from strangers? Were these the guests her father had mentioned? The adrenaline from the fight was fading and her wound throbbed as blood continued to trickle past her fingers.

Alix pressed her lips into a thin line, and her gaze searched the shadows for danger. "Meredith, I don't think—"

"I'll be fine, and if I'm not, I know you'll come running," Meredith said with a calm smile. "Now go. Hurry."

Alix scrunched up her nose with displeasure but nodded and started jogging down the road towards the plaza.

The woman turned back to Anastasia, who was still sprawled on the ground where she'd been attempting her painful crawl to safety. "Alright, then," she said as she crouched beside her. Her eyes darted up briefly, watching Alix's retreating figure. She lowered her voice. "If you'll allow it, I can heal you, but I'll have to use magic."

Magic? Fae magic? Anastasia blinked up at her. The Silvids didn't use magic—they hated magic. Or feared it? She didn't exactly know the details. Few fae stayed in Haven for long.

"Are you afraid?" Meredith asked.

"No," Anastasia said. "Do it."

Meredith nodded and held her hands against Anastasia's fingers. Blood squelched against her delicate palm. Red magic leapt across the back of Meredith's hand and Anastasia's heart caught in her throat. It looked the same as the red magic that had wrapped around the wolf-beast's limbs, but the pain lessened immediately, so Anastasia stayed calm, taking deep breaths as she watched. Meredith's dark eyes ringed with that same bright red. When she pulled away, the wound was completely closed.

Meredith blinked, and the red faded from her eyes. "Don't tell anyone," she whispered, holding a bloody finger in front of her lips. "Let's get something wrapped across—a bandage of some sort." She wiped her hands on her trousers, smearing bright red across the brown fabric. The scent of blood and the deathly reek of the wolf-beast still permeated the air. Meredith dug around in one bag of luggage they'd brought with them and pulled out a long piece of folded fabric.

"I won't tell," Anastasia said. She owed her that much for healing her. "But I don't understand. Why?"

"Why? Why what? Why did I heal you? Why do I want you to keep it a secret?" Meredith looked off in the distance, a melancholy expression stealing across her face, as she unfolded the fabric. It was a pair of soft green pants. She gestured for Anastasia to draw closer, so she did. Meredith unsheathed a blade from her thigh that Anastasia had not noticed until now. She sliced the pants along the seam, cutting away a piece of fabric, which became a square bandage, applied to her injury and fastened with scraps from the now-ruined trousers. "It's too complicated to explain in this moment, but I couldn't let you suffer when I can soothe your pain—even if the rest of Silvis would sooner watch the entirety of Kaelum bleed than use their magic. So please, don't mention this to anyone, especially not Alix—the woman who was here with me."

Anastasia nodded. "I promise."

"Good," Meredith said, pushing to her feet and offering her hand.

"What about the beast?"

Anastasia took the offered hand and stood. Her legs trembled, but her wound was truly healed. Using so much magic so quickly had drained her. Anastasia took a wobbly step forward.

Meredith released Anastasia's hand, then glanced back at the charred husk. "Yes—the beast." She frowned as she moved to the corpse and crouched at its side. She brushed her fingers through its still, shadowy fur. "Shame." With her palm, she closed the beast's eyes. "We'll just wait here then," she said and sat down by the beast. "After all," she said, gesturing to the corpse. "This is what we were looking for."

Footsteps echoed on the stone. When Anastasia looked up, she saw the fearful and familiar, golden eyes of her only friend—Shiloh, with Alix at his side, and her father's knight, Marcus, trailing after them. Shiloh's long silver hair threatened to break free of the string that held it away from his face as he rushed to her. He stumbled, gagging when the scent of beast and blood hit him like a wall. He pulled the neck of his robe up and pressed it across his face as he advanced.

"Are you okay? Are you hurt? What happened?" he asked, muffled by the robe.

"I'm fine, Shiloh," Anastasia said with a lopsided smile.

"No. I smell smoke." He reached up and wiped his fingers across her nose. When he drew them back, they were black with soot. "Reckless. You almost pushed yourself to burning again. We need to get you to Elaine. These three can deal with whatever disgusting thing you killed over there." Shiloh grabbed her wrist and pulled her arm across his shoulders, taking on her weight.

"What's Mother going to do, Shiloh? I'm fine. She'll just tell me to rest, so I might as well skip the conversation. Besides, I have a meeting to attend." Despite her words, Anastasia didn't protest as Shiloh led her down the street towards her parent's house. She hadn't particularly wanted to go to the meeting and, considering the two guests of honor were in the street with a dead beast, she had a feeling the meeting would wait.

She smiled, relaxing into Shiloh's grip, and threw a glance back at the trio still gathered around the dead beast. It was over. She'd protected Haven without dying. She considered that a successful morning, so she let her friend lead the way to her parents' house, where her mother surely would be waiting to scold her and life would go back to normal by tomorrow—a peaceful, wonderful Haven.

***

It wasn't over. Meredith frowned. "The amount of damage on the mainland is too great and too widespread for a creature this small."

Alix nodded. "Agreed, but then where are the rest? Better, who made these things? What court would send undead dogs to rip through our villages?"

Meredith blew out an exasperated breath. She opened her mouth to speak, to tell Alix again that this wasn't the work of another court or some rebel army. This was a Hollow—a creature of legend. Red eyes, shadowed fur, the black blood—all hallmarks of the Hollows from their own history. The queen would believe her. She had to believe her. She clenched her fists and looked up at Alix. "It would be best to report this to the queen before speculating further. The queen needs to see this herself. Let's get it wrapped and ready for transport. We'll meet with Commander Creon and then head back to the Capital."

There was too much at stake to wait around. Her heart raced with excitement. She'd never hoped, never dreamed, that she might see a Hollow, but here she was, if only she'd gotten here sooner. Maybe she could have saved it from its demise, somehow. But, as she held onto hope, Meredith felt certain this wouldn't be the last Hollow born in Silvis during her lifetime. This was just the beginning.

CHAPTER 4

Alix

The Haven Knight, Marcus, led Alix and Meredith back to City Hall, where Commander Creon waited. Meredith fussed over the corpse of the monster, carrying it in her arms like a prize. Alix didn't understand how her mate could withstand the burnt, rotten stench of the thing. She grimaced as they approached the building, which was another of those strange, tall stone boxes that littered the city in precise, angular ways. The stone surrounding her, cutting off her line of vision, suffocated her, leaving her on edge with the strange sensation of being watched from any number of the hundreds of windows.

"Mere," Alix said, frowning at her. "Leave the stinking monster corpse outside."

Meredith mirrored her frown, her fingers tightening on her prize for a moment longer before she nodded. "I suppose the smell is a bit strong."

"The commander appreciates your consideration. Right this way," Marcus said, taking the lead through the building with its plain stone walls and cool, reflective marble floors. Alix and Meredith followed in silence. Their footsteps clacked, echoing down the hallway. After a few turns—that Alix had already memorized just in case, they entered through double doors that opened onto a room primarily occupied by a long table and chairs.

Commander Creon, head of Haven and one of only two commanders in the queen's knighthood, sat at the head of the heavy wooden table with his fingers steepled in front of his chest. A single piece of dark hair had fallen across his wrinkled forehead. Five of his knights surrounded him—two sitting and the other three standing. His stony gaze ran the length of them both, calculating and scrutinizing. "Marcus," he said. His voice boomed through the room. "Report."

The Haven Knight that had led them into City Hall, straightened, clasping his hands behind his back, and addressed his commander, "Brigadier Alixandra Bludeg and Lady Meredith Kaesy arrived in Haven, where they found an injured knight in combat with an unidentified creature. Brigadier Bludeg sought aid, wherein she found the mage and myself. The mage took the injured knight for aid."

Commander Creon tapped his fingers together as he stared at Marcus intensely. "Identify the injured knight."

"It was the Keeper, sir. The mage took her home to Miss Elaine." Marcus dropped his eyes to the ground, his head bowing slightly as if in regret.

Commander Creon's lips pursed into a thin line. Silence hung in the air, heavy as stone. His fingers interlaced and tightened until his knuckles were nearly white and trembling. After a long moment of lingering silence, he turned his attention to Alix.

"Brigadier," he said.

"Commander," Alix responded. She and Meredith stood beside Marcus, just barely inside the room with the doors still wide open behind them.

"Did you see the creature?"

"I saw what was left of it after your daughter burnt it to a crisp."

At her words, Commander Creon's fingers relaxed slightly, and he nodded. "Describe what you saw."

Meredith stepped forward. "If I may interrupt, the creature's remains are just outside. You may see them if you wish." Alix looked between Meredith and the commander. It always made her nervous when Meredith butted in. She was too impulsive, arrogant, prideful, indirect, which all boiled down to the fact that she was too noble. Meredith was the perfect heir for the Duchess of Kaesy, but she wasn't technically a knight. Alix often wished Meredith would stop chasing the knighthood and accept her place as the Duchy's heir in place of her little sister. In moments like these, Alix admitted she didn't understand her mate at all.

Commander Creon nodded. "Yes. Let's get this over with, then, so we can adjourn this meeting."

In a few moments, they were all outside again with the corpse of the monster. The commander glared down at the beast, his face tinged red. The crowd of knights gathered around the burnt beast, most of them held the tails of their shirts against their nose and mouth. One knight who had been sitting beside Creon stood off to the side, gagging at the stench. The monster looked just as disgusting as it had before—exposed flesh, black smears of sludgy blood, matted shadows of fur.

"Cover it," Commander Creon barked and turned his attention to Alix and Meredith. "You will need to take this to Queen Harmoni to confirm her suspicions."

"Suspicions?" Meredith butted in with a strange excitement that made Alix grimace. "Did the queen ... believe the attacks to have been Hollows?"

Alix scoffed and waited for the commander to reprimand Meredith's ridiculousness, but he didn't. Commander Creon hesitated, looking around the plaza before he spoke. "Rumors have been circulating since the attack on the village in Caine." Alix knew about that attack. It had been brutal—the fae had been ripped apart, blood drained from their lifeless corpses. She'd been told no one survived. Commander Creon continued, "Queen Harmoni believes that, yes, those ancient beasts have been reborn. Because of the massacres, fear is already high across Silvis. The queen does not want to cancel the first ball of the season, so we'll need to get to the palace soon to handle this matter before the ball. We can send you with supplies for your return trip today."

Tonight? Alix bit her lower lip. That was much sooner than she'd expected, but the commander knew best.

"I'll send a party of mages along with you to set up a barrier spell around the palace. I will have the party assembled and a carriage prepared with supplies by noon. We can't risk night travel in the desert." Commander Creon rolled his shoulders back and lifted his eyes to his knights. "You are all dismissed—except you, Marcus. Meeting adjourned."

The other knights bowed their heads before dispersing to whatever duties must occupy their time in the cavernous city, while Marcus stood by the commander, who spoke to him in quick commands, ordering him to find some box to put the monster in that would contain its smell before the journey.

Meredith bent down and carefully wrapped the monster corpse back in the fabric before looking back to Alix with a wide grin that lit her face. The sudden radiance of her mate took her aback. Alix blinked hard, trying to get her bearings as the commander turned his attention back to her and Meredith.

"If you two would join me," he said. "I can offer you accommodations—a shower, perhaps, and breakfast—at my home. If you would, please, hand the creature off to Marcus, my lady." He gestured to Meredith, who hesitantly released the corpse into Marcus' waiting arms.

The knight's lips curled with disgust, but he took the stinking thing and marched off. Meredith crossed her arms and as they all began walking across the plaza, she turned her head, eyes searching for Marcus. The commander set out a grueling pace for their walk and within a minute they were at his dark, wooden door, marked with strange symbols. The house itself looked nearly identical to every other she'd walked past in Haven, though wider. Three stories of stone squished between the other buildings, while its narrow, peaked roof stretched up into the strange underground sky of Haven.

He rushed through necessary information—where to find the bathrooms, towels, the strange way their water system worked—faucets at head height that spewed water while the person stood and bathed in the constant spray of water, and where to put their luggage, that Alix had picked up in the street where they'd thoughtlessly left it. Afterwards, he quickly left them, presumably to find his injured daughter.

Meredith took the shower first, so Alix just sat on the cold stone floor in the hallway, slowly unbuckling the pieces of her leathers. Her thoughts wandered, shifting violently from disbelief and skepticism about the Hollows to her arguments with Meredith, and then to the fragile bond they shared. Alix understood nothing about mate bonds—or Hollows either, she guessed.

With a sigh, she relaxed against the wall, half undressed. Maybe Meredith was right, and she needed to read more—maybe then she'd figure out how to fix their bond that never clicked in quite right. It was supposed to be easy, wasn't it? But nothing was easy. Nothing was *ever* easy for them. The sound of running water lulled Alix's frazzled thoughts, leaving her tired and nearly asleep on the cold stone of the commander's house.

CHAPTER 5

Anastasia

Only an hour, or two at the most, had passed since Anastasia had killed the rotted wolf in the streets of Haven. Sitting on her parent's couch, in a clean set of clothes, felt wrong. Her hair, still wet from a much-needed shower, hung limp against her face. The house felt foreign. She no longer lived here. She was no longer the young girl who lived here once.

The smell of burnt flesh wouldn't leave her nose, nor would the sounds the creature made as it died. She had never killed before, not like that. She'd gone on the hunting expeditions that explored the desert, fishing on the shores, but that was for food. This? This was different. She wrapped her arms around herself, keeping a shiver at bay. It was necessary. She'd needed to protect the city. Her duty was to protect the city. She nodded to herself.

Her mother, Elaine, sat nearby chewing on her thumbnail. After being reassured multiple times by Elaine, Shiloh had finally left when Anastasia got in the shower. He had his own duty to tend to with the mage branch of the Haven Knights. So, now, Anastasia sat alone in the den with her mother, who sat and watched with a worried expression.

"I'm fine," Anastasia said, smiling at her mother. She'd kept her promise to Meredith by not telling Elaine about her healed leg, which only presented a larger problem when she had found it completely healed.

"You're not hearing any strange voices? or ..." Elaine hesitated. "Any other strange thoughts or desires?"

"No, Mother." What did Elaine think? Could the strange wolf-beasts turn someone's mind with their bite? Anastasia longed to put her armor back on to do something normal just to chase thoughts of the morning away.

"And your magic? It feels normal?" Elaine shifted to the couch beside Anastasia and pressed a hand to her forehead.

"I'm fine. It's fine. What do you know about the creature I ..." *killed*. "Fought?"

"Creature?" Elaine pulled away and raised her brows. "Oh. I have no clue about any of that. Was it not just a stray wolf or some other creature?"

"Then why are you fussing so much and asking so many strange questions?" Anastasia slid away, turning to face her mother.

Elaine raised her thumb to her lips again for a moment before dropping it. "The flames are a curse as much as they are a blessing."

"Yes. I know—Using too much magic and I'll burn from the inside out," Anastasia said with a sigh, repeating the admonishment she'd heard all her life.

"Darling," Elaine said, patting Anastasia's knee. "It's a bit more complicated than that. You need to be more careful. I don't want to lose you to the flames."

"I'm not burning. I'm fine," she said again.

On the other side of the house, the door slammed shut. Voices carried through the house, faded, and then heavy footsteps pounded down the stairs.

Elaine patted Anastasia on the cheek. "Look's like your father is home," she said.

"Anastasia?!" her father called.

"We're in here, Cree," her mother said, raising her voice to be heard through the walls.

Her father's ragged countenance appeared in the doorway, and his eyes immediately latched onto Anastasia. He took two quick steps forward and then paused. "Marcus reported on the incident," he said. "You were injured?"

"Just a scratch," Anastasia said with a shrug. "I'm fine." At least she was now that Meredith had healed her. The blood loss still made her feel a bit unsteady, but they didn't need to know that.

"Good," he said. His shoulders relaxed with a long exhale.

"It was certainly more than a scratch," Elaine said. "There was so much blood all over your trousers and tunic." She turned to Creon with a pointed look. "She nearly burned and whatever *scratch* she had was completely healed by the time I saw it."

Anastasia opened her mouth to protest, wishing she could explain, but she couldn't—wouldn't—break her promise to Meredith. She was fine. What was the big deal? She hadn't used too much of her magic.

Creon tightened his lips with displeasure. "Has she—?"

Elaine shook her head. "No, but I think we need to be more careful."

Creon nodded. "Then, it'd be best if she stay with me while you work on more protection sigils."

"Why do you both insist on talking as if I'm not sitting in the same room?" Anastasia pushed her fingers into her brows, rubbing her face in frustration. "I survived. I know my limits," *now*.

"Oh, sweetie," Elaine said, pulling Anastasia into a hug as they sat together on the couch. "We're just worried about you. I wish you didn't have to carry the burden of the Keeper."

"I'm fine," she said again, but her voice was small and quiet. She almost didn't believe herself. Their fear felt like a shadow in the room, creeping around her and stealing her breath.

"Fine enough to go on a mission with me?" Creon asked. Elaine gave him a hard stare, but Anastasia paid her no attention. A mission was exactly what she needed. She needed to throw herself into something, to escape from the sounds, the images, the fear.

"Cree, do you really think that's a good idea?" Elaine asked.

His eyes softened as he looked at his wife. "She'll be with me. It'll be the best way to watch for *signs*."

"Alright, then," Elaine said with a worried sigh.

"What mission?" Anastasia asked, ignoring the needless worry of her family. She would be careful next time. She wouldn't let herself burn through her soul.

Creon sat rigidly on the edge of a recliner. "I'll be escorting the fae back to the palace ... and there will be a ball."

"A fae ball? You want me to attend a fae ball?" Anastasia blinked at him incredulously.

"Only briefly. The main objective is to reinforce the protective barriers around the palace. It is highly probable that the creature you fought is not the only one, and with the nobles of Silvis flocking to the palace, safety is a priority." He shifted back and forth on the chair, running his hand across his dry knuckles. "You need more practice with sigils and all the other ways to use the flame without pulling it from within you. I'll need to set up some time for a mage to teach you runes and sigils."

Practice. That made more sense. Her father wasn't the type to indulge in frivolities, especially not a fae ball. He was right, though. She needed the practice. Pulling magic from the environment using channels, like words and sigils, was a much safer way to cast than what she normally did, which pulled the magic from her own soul to fuel the spells.

"Alright," Anastasia said. "I'll go."

"Good. We're leaving at noon."

Noon? That wasn't remotely enough time to get ready. "I don't have a dress," was all that came out of Anastasia's mouth.

Creon pushed up from his chair. "I'll send someone ahead of us by horse to get a dressmaker started on something for you. We'll arrive in plenty of time to have everything arranged. Just get your things ready for travel and we'll head out from City Hall at noon." He glanced back at Elaine. "I trust you'll handle everything else."

"Of course," Elaine said before putting a hand on Anastasia's arm. "Let's go get you ready, dear."

"Alright," she said, standing with her mother's help, while her father nodded and left them to their preparations.

Anastasia still kept some of her things here at her parents' house, so it didn't take long to pack travel bags from her old clothes. Excitement buzzed through her. A fae ball. She'd always wanted to dance, to see the fae dance, to just exist for a moment in the splendor, and now she finally would.

CHAPTER 6

Anastasia

Noon came sooner than Anastasia expected. The company, made up of her father, Anastasia, the two fae women, Shiloh, and a handful of knights and mages, travelled by carriage through the Silvid Desert, then across the Abyssal Bay to the mainland of Silvis. They docked at Queen's Creek just as night was falling and took fresh horses and carriages along the road to the Capital. They hadn't stopped at all during the night, only pausing on their journey in the morning for breakfast and a change of horses at a small knight outpost before taking the road north.

The journey had been quiet. The empty roads surprised Anastasia, but then again, she didn't leave the desert often, so she had nothing to compare it to other than the bustle of Haven. She hadn't been able to sleep much during their nighttime travel.

Now, it was nearing noon again and Shiloh slept, crumpled in the carriage's corner. She was glad her father had at least indulged her in this. He'd refused to let her ride horseback, citing her fight with the Hollow. "Exhaustion," he had said, "cannot be allowed atop a horse, Anastasia." He wouldn't ride in the carriage with her though—he had to oversee the knights, so instead, he'd allowed Shiloh, brought along as a mage for the mission, to keep her company. She rarely saw him these days, and when she did, he was almost always barely awake. She wondered what the Haven Mages were forcing him to do. What grueling training did they put their mages through?

The carriage rolled to a stop in a tree-lined meadow, interrupting her thoughts. The first touches of autumn streaked the forest with shades of orange and yellow, mixed with the vibrant green of live oaks and pine. Anastasia stared with a giddy excitement at the landscape she'd only ever seen in paintings.

She heard her father's voice calling for a lunch break—the last break before they'd reach the Capital. Anticipation made her stomach twist in knots.

Shiloh jerked awake as the door to their carriage snapped open. Books he'd been reading at various points in the journey fell to the floor as he scrambled into a sitting position, eyes wide.

"Anastasia," her father's voice boomed into the carriage. "While the horses and knights rest, you are to learn sigils." He turned his attention to Shiloh. "Specifically, the sigil to reserve magic from the environment and the ignition sigil."

"Yes, sir," Shiloh said, bowing his head.

Before Anastasia could speak, her father closed the carriage door and walked off, barking orders to the rest of the company.

"Alright, then Shi. What do I do?"

Shiloh rubbed a hand across his face and untied the ribbon in his hair. The silver locks fell around his face. "Well, we can't practice in the carriage unless you have a desire for arson, so I suppose the first order of business is to get out of this horrendous contraption." He combed his fingers through hair before tying it back again.

"Take the lead," she said, gesturing to the carriage door.

Shiloh grabbed a book and pushed out of the carriage, nearly tumbling in eagerness to escape. Anastasia suppressed a laugh. The ride hadn't been pleasant, but Shiloh's obvious hatred was unexpected. She followed behind him and he led her to a clearing a suitable distance away from the trees and everyone else.

He sat on the ground, his pale robes flaring around him in the grass. "Have you ever used sigils? Or have any prior knowledge?" he asked, already flipping through the book in his hand.

"I know the basics, I guess, but I've never actually... used one. Not really." Anastasia fidgeted with the chainmail tasset resting against her thigh as she sat on the ground in front of Shiloh.

He glanced up from the book with a raised brow. "What do you consider the basics, Ana?"

"Um, well…" She hated learning theory. It always made her feel like an idiot. "Sigils and spoken spells are channels for magic that use the energy in the environment."

"Instead of the magical energy within your soul. Yes," he said, looking down at the book again. He tapped the page, gesturing for her to take notice of the sigil on the page. It looked like a series of squiggling lines. "This is a rune. Runes are words. Words are power." He flipped the page.

A circle filled with the runes took up the entire page. He tapped each rune as he spoke, naming them—draw, essence, hold. "Runes form a sigil, bound by a circle. It directs the users' intention and the magic of Faerie gives it life."

Anastasia nodded. She knew this—at least, she vaguely remembered being taught this before. "What's this sigil for, then?"

"What do you think it's for?" Shiloh asked.

Anastasia suppressed a groan. She didn't want to think, but Shiloh wouldn't let her slide by, barely understanding this. He worried as much as her father did. She studied the sigil again. Draw, essence, hold. "Pulling and holding essence?" She guessed.

Shiloh tilted his head to the side, evaluating her answer. "Yes, but what is essence?"

She turned the word over in her mind. It had no meaning for her. "The elements? Nature? The spirit of something?"

Shiloh grinned and tapped his nose. "Spirit. That's close. Close enough, anyway." His golden eyes were brighter than she'd seen them in years. Her heart ached for him. Once this was all over, she should insist he have a vacation from his duties with the mages. He needed a break.

"The most direct translation from the runic is actually 'soul,' but most textbooks prefer essence. Too many debates over the ethicality of using the soul of Faerie to fuel magic. Though obviously ethics has stopped no mages and we're not the only ones to use sigils, so..." Anastasia stared at him blankly, barely processing his quick words, critiquing the semantics of magic academia.

He paused, waving his hand in the air as if the dispel the lecture Anastasia hadn't even heard. "Anyway," he said. "The rune for essence is used to target magic in the environment, so this sigil is to draw magic from the world, then hold it in reserve—within the sigil—until it's needed."

He pulled a small, leather-bound notebook from a pocket of his robes and a pencil and handed it to Anastasia. "Practice drawing this until you can do it from memory. Once you have it—and the ignition sigil—memorized, we'll worry about actually teaching you to activate the sigils."

Anastasia gripped the pencil, glaring at the page. Shiloh spread out in the grass and took another nap while she labored over the notebook. The company stayed in the meadow for nearly three hours and in that time, she'd barely been able to memorize the first sigil.

At Shiloh's insistence, she spent the rest of their afternoon journey in the carriage hunched over the notebook, repeating the two sigils over and over again. After ten of each sigil in a row without looking at the book, she sighed, smiling her victory over at Shiloh.

He nodded. "Once we're settled in the commander's Capital estate, we'll begin the next part of your lesson."

Anastasia's fingers ached, and she tossed the notebook and pencil onto the bench beside Shiloh, glad to be free from his teaching. She turned her attention to the window, watching as the Capital slowly took shape in the distance. Her earlier excitement returned in full force. She'd finally see the fae Capital of Silvis. Her daydreams filled the rest of the carriage ride with pleasant thoughts of the ball to come.

CHAPTER 7

Anastasia

The late afternoon sun hung low in the sky, painting the sky in a rush of gold and crimson. Anastasia squinted her eyes against the light, eager to see the Capital for the first time. The carriage rattled along cobblestone roads through fields of waving grainl. A stone wall surrounded the Capital, which their company passed through with no trouble from the knights guarding the wide entrance.

Anastasia took in every detail she could as the carriage made its way through the city. The houses were a wave of brown, unlike Haven's stony depths. Here, cozy cottages made of wood lined the cobble streets and the golden warmth of natural fires glowed in the windows. Street lamps clicked on as the sun continued its descent, bathing the surroundings with a strange yellow glow. Anastasia narrowed her eyes at the lamps. She knew fire like she knew her own breath. The flickering of the yellow lamps was not fire.

Strange. Beautiful and strange.

Despite the beauty of the Capital and her own curiosity, she missed the comfort of stone beneath her feet and all around her, hiding her from the sky and its harsh sun. The carriage slowed and iron gates opened with a rusted squeal. She pushed her face against the window. She had finally arrived at her father's estate.

The estate seemed enormous to Anastasia, even though it wasn't nearly as large as the mansions further down the road. She knew the estate existed, but she'd never seen it. The queen had given him the home when he'd accepted the position of commander in her knighthood despite already being the leader of Haven. Her father had never even described the place.

Unlike the cottages she'd passed, the manor was mostly gray stone. Four peaks rose at the front of the roof, like small mountains above curved windows. Though beautiful, the jumbled shapes of the building looked like four separate homes shoved together. A pond took up one corner of the manicured yard, nestled beside another, much smaller, stone building.

The carriage bumped down the drive, halting in front of the manor. An older woman, plump and smiling broadly, stood with her hands clasped, her gray hair in a neat bun, revealing the roundness of her ears. She was human, which surprised Anastasia. She thought all humans lived in Haven.

Creon stopped before the woman and dismounted from his horse. Anastasia shook Shiloh's shoulder, who had fallen asleep again after they'd eaten a very late lunch in the carriage. Once certain he was awake, she eagerly pushed the carriage door open and stumbled out.

"Yes, that would be preferable," Creon said to the older woman, who was nodding with warm exuberance.

"Lovely. Just wonderful," she said, clapping her hands together in front of her chest. The woman's eyes jumped to where Anastasia now stood, stretching from the intense travel. "That must be her, then? Oh, what a dear. She'll be beautiful."

Creon grunted in the affirmative before speaking, "Do as you will, then." He turned to the knights awaiting his orders and began barking directions—a few to help with stabling the horses, a knight for luggage, and a knight with him to assess the estate.

As the rest of their party—a handful of mages, Shiloh, the knights, and the two fae women—started settling in, Anastasia found herself at the mercy of the grinning woman. "Hello, my dear!" She said, beaming. "Your father has a wonderful surprise for you—a dress. Oh, my, you'll be such a darling doll. Come." The woman beckoned her forward into the house, humming as she went. "Anastasia, yes?"

"Yes?" Anastasia said hesitantly. Her boots barely made a sound on the thick rugs that lined the wooden floors. Candles flickered invitingly on low tables and a candelabra stood in several corners, casting its familiar glow. The exposed stone walls comforted Anastasia. In Haven, the stone was smooth, but here the walls were interlocking brick. She dragged her fingers along the stone.

An enormous chandelier of silver hung in the center of the foyer, emitting that strange yellow light, but Anastasia didn't have time to stare at the contraption as the woman left her behind, picking up a quick pace.

"That's the name you go by? No Nickname? Such a beautiful name," the woman said, babbling on with a happy ease. Anastasia rushed after her, disappointed that she had to ignore the paintings and other decorations that hung about the manor.

"Oh, well, Mother used to call me Little Ana—Lil'Ana, but I don't suppose that's what you meant. Anastasia is fine... or Ana." Her cheeks heated, feeling embarrassed by her own admissions.

The woman laughed. "Lil'Ana, how sweet." She fluttered a hand against her heart. "Your room is just around the corner."

"Ma'am? I didn't catch your name..." Anastasia said, following the woman around the corner and through a set of carved wooden doors and into a dark bedroom.

"No? My word. I'm such a goose, aren't I?" she said, gesturing Anastasia further into the room. She could barely make out shapes—a bed in the center of the room, bedside tables, a couch in the corner by a curtained window. "I'm Luna Graye, the head maid—well, only maid, actually. We don't get visitors. Even the commander isn't often in residence. Jerald and I keep the place in working order and our son keeps the horses."

Luna brushed her hand across the wall, flicking a switch. Light burst into the room—the same yellow glow of the street lamps and chandelier. Anastasia narrowed her eyes at the source of the light, a sphere hanging from the ceiling.

"Miss Graye, what's that?" Anastasia pointed at the light.

Luna raised her brows. "Miss? My word," she chuckled. "Just call me Luna. Do you mean the light?"

"Yes. We have nothing like that in Haven. Is it magic?"

Luna pressed her palms against her chest again and widened her eyes. "No, of course not. We would never—to think—" she shook her head, fumbling with her words. "Dear Celestials. Do you not have electricity in Haven?"

Anastasia frowned. "I don't even know what that is."

Luna grinned, chuckling good-naturedly as she began bustling about the room again, smoothing the curtains to keep the afternoon light out. "The academy invented these wonderful devices who knows how long ago," she said. "But look! At the flick of a switch, you have light." To demonstrate, Luna touched the switch on the wall again, dropping the room back into darkness, before turning the light on again.

"I just can't believe the commander wouldn't have electricity installed. Baffling really," Luna muttered to herself.

Anastasia grimaced. She really didn't want to talk about her father, so she changed the subject. "You said it's just you, your husband, and son. It's only the three of you taking care of this big house?" Anastasia asked.

"Well, yes, most of the time. When the commander visits, we bring in a few temporary hands. My sister-in-law runs a maid service. Quite convenient, really." Luna leaned on one leg, tilting sideways to peek through a door at the far end of the room. "Oh, wonderful! It's already been delivered." She rushed inside, leaving Anastasia alone in the bedroom.

After a few moments, she waddled out, holding a dress up above her head to keep the bottom from dragging the ground. At least, Anastasia assumed the fluffy wad of red fabric spilling from Luna's hands was a dress. The fabric shimmered softly in the strange light of the room. She draped the dress carefully across the bed, smoothing the fabric and fluffing the skirts.

"Oh, look at those little suns," Luna said as her hands fluttered across the fabric, fingers tracing the gold lace suns that hid behind a transparent red tulle. Anastasia couldn't deny it was beautiful, but ... still, she felt her heart twisting in knots. It wasn't what she'd imagined when she dreamed of attending a fae ball. Everything about the dress screamed Haven—diplomat, outsider.

Anastasia wanted to disappear into the crowd, to feel like part of the rush of noble fae. She forced a smile to her face. She was being too harsh. It was a beautiful dress, and she loved Haven. She'd never been to a fae ball—maybe she would look the part, look like every other person there.

Luna clicked her tongue in thought. "Before tomorrow, I'll likely need to make some alterations. You'll need to try it on."

Anastasia grimaced. She really had no desire to put the dress on at the moment. All she really wanted to do was go to sleep. She hated travelling. It always made her feel sick. "But–" Anastasia began, but Luna interrupted.

"I'll need to find my sewing pouch. Why don't you go fetch some dinner and take a bath first? I'll come to find you, dear," she said, nodding to herself. Luna exited the room with a backward wave, rushing to her tasks without giving Anastasia even a moment to speak.

She was alone again, feeling exposed in the strange environment. But Luna was right, she should go eat something and there were still sigil lessons with Shiloh. Perhaps food and a bath would settle her stomach, or at least soothe the uneasiness that clung to her skin.

CHAPTER 8

Meredith

Meredith reclined on a lounge in one of the many rooms of the commander's house in the Capital. After all the travelling, she had no desire to have discussions with Creon, but propriety meant she had no choice. Alix paced the room, rolling her shoulders now and then. Her mate prowled like a caged predator. Subconsciously, Meredith sought the golden thread of their bond, which coiled deep in her chest. The warmth of that connection soothed her. She'd read that mates were empathic through the bond, some even telepathic, but her and Alix's thread was ... wrong, somehow—not frayed, not broken. It felt slightly off kilter—a guitar string not set properly in its groove.

Meredith focused on that thread, caressing it with her mind, willing it to fall into place. The creaking door and swishing skirts broke her reverie, alerting her to an unexpected guest's arrival.

Queen Harmoni, dressed in flowing silver skirts and her brown hair braided into a pile on top of her head, entered the library. Meredith scrambled to her feet and Alix moved to her side, pulling her up with ease.

Meredith slipped into a curtsey while Alix bowed beside her. "Hello, Your Majesty," Meredith said.

"Your Majesty," Alix echoed.

"Rise," said the queen. Commander Creon followed the queen into the room, pulling a chair out for her at a nearby table. She gestured for them to come sit with her at the table as she sat down. "I'm afraid we've entered an unfortunate time." With an elbow on the table and her hand delicately arranged across her jaw, one finger against the corner of her lips, she waited to continue until Meredith, Alix, and Creon had taken seats at the table. "Will the Keeper not join us, Commander?"

Creon stiffened for a fraction of an instant before shifting in his chair. "She is taking lessons with the mages in preparation for the ball tomorrow, Your Majesty, but if you desire her presence, I will fetch her for you."

The queen waved a hand dismissively, shaking her head. "I cannot linger here at your estate. Our meeting will need to wait, it seems."

"I apologize, Your Majesty." Creon bowed his head and the queen merely nodded before speaking again.

The queen pursed her lips, looking at the three sitting around the table. "I hesitate to speak the words, but I must."

She inhaled deeply and spoke. "I have seen the..." The queen paused, when she spoke again it was with a grimace.

"Evidence you have brought, which confirms the Hollows have returned to Silvis." Her words hung in the air with a sense of finality that only left Meredith's heart racing with excitement. The legends were real. Meredith had to bite her tongue to keep from exclaiming.

The queen turned to Meredith. "Your mother and I have recently spoken of your academic interest. Have you actually read all the texts on Hollows in the main palace library? Even the ones written in Old Silvid?"

"Yes, I have," Meredith said in a breathless rush.

"And Brigadier Bludeg, you come highly recommended—and not just by your father," she said with a small smile.

"You flatter me, my queen." Alix bowed again. Meredith wondered what Alix could be thinking. Was she pleased with the words? Did she still think she wasn't good enough to live beyond her father's shadow? Meredith forced her shoulders to relax as she focused on the queen's next words.

"Considering you two are inseparable, I have need of you with this problem." The queen sat back in her chair, folding her hands in her lap. "From the pattern of attacks, it seems the Hollows are heading towards Abyssal Bay—the Hollow you found in Haven, makes me think they are congregating in the desert. I intend to send you two, along with some knights from the Capital, for an extended stay in Haven—as you requested, commander. You are to discover why they are being drawn to the desert," the queen hesitated, tapping her nails on the arm of the chair. "Unless absolutely necessary for the investigation, eliminate any Hollow you encounter."

Eliminate. The word echoed painfully in Meredith's head, but she nodded. "Yes, my queen." She wouldn't go against the queen's orders, but hope still fluttered. If she could make keeping them alive necessary for their investigation, she could avoid the needless death of these legendary creatures.

The queen stood, and the three rose with her. "Commander, I trust you will handle the specifics of getting everything settled?"

"Yes, Your Majesty," he said.

"Good." The queen turned to leave, but Meredith took several quick steps after her.

"Wait!" She held up her hand, reaching out towards the queen. "My queen."

The queen stopped and turned an ear towards Meredith.

"In my readings, there are mentions of other texts—ones I've never found. Are there, perhaps, any that aren't publicly available? I believe it will help with our task."

The queen tilted her head, eyes lifted to the ceiling in thought. "Perhaps. I'll have Athan look through the private libraries. I'll see you all at the ball." With that, the queen exited the room in a rush of glittering fabric and clicking footsteps.

Commander Creon crossed his arms as he looked between Alix and Meredith. "Lady Meredith, I need a word."

Meredith furrowed her brows with confusion and glanced at Alix before returning her attention to the commander. "What could you possibly desire to speak to me about? Alix is a higher military rank than I."

He shook his head. "This has nothing to do with military strategy or the investigation. I need to speak to you about Anastasia's injury," he said.

Meredith's heart jumped into her throat. What did he know? Had Anastasia told him the truth of her secret? She laughed, trying to sound relieved and comfortable. "Of course. I was the first to look after her wound, so it only makes sense that you would need my insight, as a medic, while she continues to heal. Alix?" Meredith turned, forcing her face into a pleasant mask. "I'll meet you at dinner shortly. Shall we go for a walk, commander?"

Alix narrowed her eyes, and Meredith knew Alix was attempting to see through her to the truth. She wouldn't let her. Meredith smiled softly and offered Commander Creon her arm. "A stroll through the garden?"

The commander raised his brows, but took her arm. Meredith took the lead, stretching her long stride to put distance between herself and Alix. She wasn't ready to reveal her secret to her mate, who hated magic so deeply. She couldn't take the rejection, so she walked away.

***

Meredith smelled the faint scent of roses on the wind as she and the commander sat on benches across from each other in the garden. The glow of the sun had finally disappeared beyond the horizon, leaving the manor in the comfortable darkness of dusk. Stars began to appear in the sky, but Meredith did not notice the surrounding beauty. Her heart pounded in her ears much too hard for her to focus on anything else.

"What is it you wanted to discuss, commander?" Meredith whispered.

"Secrets, I suppose," he said with a sigh.

Meredith's breath hitched and her voice squeaked as she said, "secrets?" she chuckled, but the sound quivered in the air with her nerves.

"I saw the blood—my daughter's blood —and yet there is no wound."

Meredith's thoughts spun. Should she make excuses for the blood? Should she fake surprise? What if she just admitted to the truth? Fear tightened its hold on her heart, but the thought of confession, finally speaking it of her own accord without someone's life or death on the line, forcing her hand. The thought made her lightheaded.

"Families are full of secrets, buried with time, hidden from the people we care about most," he said, running a shaky hand through his hair.

"Yes," Meredith whispered, afraid to say more, though a hopeful part of her heart yearned for freedom. If Creon found out, what would happen? Would Alix find out or the queen? Would all the cards fall in the fragile house she'd made, finally letting her stop lying to cover who she was underneath it all?

"Is it true?" he asked. "Her miraculous healing?"

Meredith counted the beat of her heart.

One. Two. Could she admit to it? Could she handle the fallout?

Three. Would Alix choose her? Love her? Despite her hatred of magic?

Four. Could she even lie anymore? Could she pretend to be something she wasn't?

Five. He already knew. The queen must already know, and yet she hadn't said a word in their meeting.

Six. If the queen could accept her, Alix surely would. Seven.

Meredith took a deep breath and exhaled slowly. "Yes. It's true. I healed her."

Commander Creon sat up straight and stared at Meredith. His mouth parted slightly, breath wheezing out in a sudden gust. "What? No. Wait—hold on. You?"

Meredith's eyes widened. What was this reaction? "You knew, didn't you? That's why you asked me?" *Oh no. Oh no. Had she made a mistake?*

"Knew? Knew that you were using Silvid magic when the whole of Silvis would condemn you for it? Of course not," he laughed dryly. "I would have never guessed one of the highest fae nobles of Silvis would even know how to use that ancient magic."

"I—I... no. I don't understand. Why did you call me out here?" Meredith's eyes darted around the garden, looking in every shadow for listening ears or prying eyes. She relaxed slightly. No one was lurking in the dark to hear her whispered secret. "Please don't tell anyone," she pleaded, hating herself for how quickly she clung to her lies again. She was sick of lying about magic, but he was right. The whole of Silvis, the queen and, more importantly, Alix, would hate her gift.

"I would never," he swore. "You saved my daughter, though it put you at a significant risk. I'll keep your secret."

"How can I trust that you'll do as you say?" Meredith wrapped her arms around herself, bristling against the chill wind that blew through the garden.

"If my word is not enough, my lady, then I'll give you a secret of my own. Will that suffice?"

A secret for a secret, so they were both ready at a moment's notice to blackmail the other? "It seems you know the ways of the nobles, commander. That will suffice."

"My family bears the soul of a dragon," he said. His shoulders slumped and his head fell into his hands. "I should alone bear the burden, but when Anastasia was born, the voice of the dragon faded, disappeared. I can barely call the flames as I had once been able to. I fear the dragon has chosen a new vessel in my daughter and she's completely unaware of this or our family history."

Dragons. Meredith nodded. A secret indeed. For centuries, dragons inspired fear. The Summer Court—the court of dragons—was among the most powerful fae in all the Faerie realms.

In ancient times, war had broken out among the natural dragons and the fae. The War of Dragons had lasted centuries in the Summer Court, ultimately ending in a treaty that bound the fae of the Summer Court to the dragons. Since then, dragon souls joined with the souls of fae, granting them power and the ability to shift, while the dragons had avoided extinction and continued to have dominion over the land, through the royal lines of the Summer Court.

Meredith pressed her fingers to her lips. This was a secret indeed. To harbor a dragon soul within a human body made them ... "A descendant of the Summer Court royal fae."

The commander lifted his head and met her gaze. "I tell you this now, not only to gain your trust, but to also ask you for help. If the dragon wakes, I fear what will become of her."

Though a descendant of the fae, Anastasia had a human body and mind. Meredith leaned back, tilting her head to the stars. She'd read of the dragons—what noble child hadn't been fascinated by them? Their shifts were sudden, explosive, painful. A dragon soul was a dominating presence. Many fae even lost their minds to the dragon within them. If Anastasia, a mere human, were to shift, she may never regain her self again.

"Elaine and I have put precautions in place. We continue to research contingency plans in case symptoms appear. If the dragon rears its head within her, I will do everything within my power to quell the beast before it can consume her," he said. "Do I have your silence as you have mine?"

"Yes," she said. Hollows and now dragons? Legends were alive in front of Meredith's eyes. She could barely believe it.

"Will you help me?"

"In what way?" Meredith asked.

"Watch her. I cannot be with her at all times. I realize you cannot either, but help me watch her for signs of the dragon."

Meredith furrowed her brows as she took in the commander's haggard expression. She barely knew him or his daughter, but they were the only ones who knew her secret. What a wonderful and terrifying thing it was to her — honesty.

"What sort of signs?" she asked.

"Maybe I should explain a bit better," he said, rubbing a hand through his hair again.

"Yes, please," she said as she settled back on the bench again. The metal bit into her legs, chilling through the thin fabric of her dress.

"I'm not sure if it's similar for the fae of the Summer Court, but for those dragon-bearers in Haven, the dragon's soul is separate from ours. It's like…" he held his clenched fists in front of himself, pressing them together. "Two bubbles pressing against each other. When the dragon-bearer uses their magic, the line between those bubbles begins to erode. If the mage were to use too much magic, and end up burning themselves out, the line disappears completely."

"So burning causes the souls to merge?"

He relaxed his fists until his fingers intertwined completely. "Yes, but there are signs even before a complete burn," he said. "Soot at the orifices. The smell of smoke on her. She might hear the dragon's voice in her head. Unnaturally quick healing. Fainting. Strange urges or desires that are out of character for her. Our family's dragon is a glutton, so if her appetite changes significantly even that could be a sign."

Creon continued talking, whispering in a rush of quick words. "We've been hiding sigils of dampening and restraint on Anastasia's armor, weapons, clothes, and even her apartment for years, but it's not enough. No matter how much her mother and I warn, beg, and plead, she's reckless with her magic."

"Why not just tell Anastasia?" Surely, the girl would understand the dire circumstances if she knew the truth of her lineage.

Creon let out a short, harsh laugh that was utterly devoid of mirth. "Tell her? You don't know my daughter well, I see. Telling her would be giving her a new weapon, especially now that we are on the cusp of a war with those monsters. Anastasia takes her role as the Keeper seriously. If she knew the power hiding within her, she would wake the dragon herself if it meant saving her people."

Meredith nodded. Even in the brief time she'd known her, she could see that spark in Anastasia, the need to care for others, her stubbornness. She'd nearly died fighting that Hollow in Haven, and was crawling in the streets instead of screaming for help. Meredith believed him, so that only left her with one option. "I'll help you," she said.

"Then, we're allies?"

"I suppose we are," she said with a grin. Now, there were two people in all of Silvis she wouldn't have to lie to.

CHAPTER 9

Anastasia

The night and morning had gone much too quickly. Already, Anastasia sat in the carriage on the way to the ball.

The palace of the Court of Dreams rose in the distance as the company from Haven approached. Anastasia's father had insisted they take carriages, but she would rather be on horseback, even in this ridiculous dress. She fisted her hands nervously in the billowing skirts. She felt like a walking Haven flag—all red and gold with tiny lace suns.

Anastasia glared through the tiny windows, where her father, Commander Creon, rode alongside Alix, who wore a dress that was more armor than dress. The other soldiers and mages rode in formation around the carriage. At least she didn't have to make small talk, Anastasia thought, glancing back to the two silent occupants that rode along with her—Lady Maia and her daughter Meredith. The two talked amongst themselves. Anastasia did her best not to listen, but concluded that Lady Maia planned to marry Meredith off to some nobleman and tonight was imperative for her plans.

When the carriage finally stopped in the sweeping gardens before the palace, Anastasia was well beyond eager to escape. Dusk had already come and gone. Only the twinkling of hanging lanterns and torches lit the path. Lady Maia and Meredith exited first, with Alix chasing Meredith into the churning ballroom beyond the open doors.

Anastasia stepped out with the help of a palace hand and her eyes swept the shadows, imagining gleaming teeth looming in the night. Her eyes strained to find any flickering danger, but despite her unease, Anastasia found nothing hiding in the dark corners of the palace grounds. Images of her fight with the Hollow rose to the surface unbidden—black blood splattering the ground, dripping jaws, red eyes. She shivered, pushing those thoughts away and taking comfort in the heavy weight of her dagger hidden on her thigh beneath her dress.

Her father took her hand, drawing her attention back to the open doors, which he promptly led her through.

"Smile, at least," her father said.

Anastasia realized then that, lost in her thoughts, she must have been grimacing. She took a deep breath and offered a wide smile to her father, who pursed his lips and turned away.

Through the enormous palace doors, the ball awaited. Raucous laughter and an overwhelming buzz of noise assaulted Anastasia as she entered. Her father led her off to the side, reminding her that he would come find her when she was needed—until then, she was to smile sweetly and chat with the noble fae. After all, good relations between the humans and fae were imperative to Haven's safety. After that, he disappeared into the crowd, leaving her alone among strangers.

Moments later, trumpets blared, and a servant called out to the crowd, "Presenting Queen Harmoni and King Consort Theoden."

Two more servants pulled open the grand doors at the back of the room. Anticipatory silence settled. Then, with beaming smiles, the queen and king of Silvis entered the room to fervent applause. Even a few chants of "long live our beloved queen" broke out for a moment as the pair glided through the crowd to their thrones, which sat only slightly raised, just barely apart from the rest of the festivities.

Before sitting, the queen smiled at her subjects, sweet and adoring. Even Anastasia felt swept up in admiration for Queen Harmoni.

"With much delight, I would like to present your crown prince, Vasileios," Queen Harmoni said.

The room fell silent, gasps following the announcement. Of course, Anastasia knew there was a prince, but she'd never seen him. In fact, she'd heard that the prince was a recluse. No one ever saw him, even now a heavy cloak shrouded him and covered his head.

The room remained silent as they all took in his figure—tall, but lithe, with stone gray skin and curling silver hair that fell across his face. He didn't smile. Anastasia thought he looked terrified, and the thought amused her. A prince, terrified? What a strange thing to be in the safest place of all Silvis, surrounded by guards who would die before letting harm come to him.

A smattering of claps rang out that slowly became a roar of applause. Anastasia couldn't look away from the prince. She tried to rationalize her interest. Was it because he looked so different from the other fae? Or that she'd never seen him before? Or perhaps her intrigue was merely because he was a prince. Despite her attempts to justify her unfamiliar feelings for him, her excuses proved unconvincing. She felt drawn to him, inexplicably and irrevocably tied to him, and that worried Anastasia more than anything ever had before.

"Let us begin the season!" the queen cried. Music swelled, and the fae twirled around the room. Their expensive, brightly-colored clothes, like blossoming flowers swaying in the breeze. Soon everyone but Anastasia forgot about the prince entirely. She watched him as he slipped into the crowd and found a shadowy corner to hide in.

Anastasia moved in the outskirts, keeping her eyes on him as she approached. He leaned against a marble pillar, clearly deep in thought. The music shifted, movements around her changed, but Anastasia paid no mind.

She stood still, captivated by the fae prince before her. He watched the ballroom with a slight frown and she felt the irrational urge to run to him, to say something ridiculous if only to make him laugh. Without meaning to, she crept closer to him. Did he envy the dancers? If it would make him smile, she would dance with him.

She was mere steps away from the prince when she finally spoke. "Would you like to dance?" she asked.

The prince jerked towards her voice, his eyes wide. This close, Anastasia could more clearly see his face. His eyes were green, bright like the grass bathed in sun that she'd seen on the carriage ride to the Capital. He kept the hood of his cloak pulled tight around his head. Curious. She wondered if his eyes were sensitive to the lights. Did he have a bad haircut? Why else would he still wear a hood in the middle of a ballroom?

Despite her curiosity, she wouldn't ask. He could tell her when he was ready, if ever. Though she hoped she might get to know him well enough, eventually. *Eventually*. The word thundered in her chest and she refused to think about the implications of her own thoughts.

Instead, she smiled hesitantly, twisting her hands nervously in her skirts. His eyes took her in, surprise shifting to curiosity, especially when he noticed her ears. She wondered if he'd ever met a human, but quickly dismissed the thought. He must have. Vasileios was the prince, after all. He'd probably seen a great many things that Anastasia had only wondered about.

"I know it may seem strange, but you just seemed so..." she trailed off and despite the anxious racing of her heart, she held out her hand. "You were watching the others so intently, I thought perhaps you might like to ... dance," she said.

A slow smile settled on his face, and he stepped towards her. Without words, he slid his palm against hers. The softness of his hands surprised her, and she feared he might find her rough, calloused palms disgusting, but he didn't pull away.

"I'm Anastasia," she whispered, hesitantly drawing closer to him.

The prince stared at her for a long moment, searching her face. "My name is Vasileios," he said.

What was he looking for in her expression? Anastasia furrowed her brow for a moment before banishing her thoughts. It didn't matter. She realized now that while she had offered to dance with him, she didn't know any of the dances. Her father had neglected that part of his plan, apparently.

A prince and a warrior, she thought, standing in the shadows of a royal ball. "It's so lonely on the edges of the excitement, but I must admit I don't actually know the court dances. My father is more interested in training me for wars, rather than dances."

Anastasia expected him to pull away, or to at least be taken aback by her comment about wars. He didn't. Instead, the prince smiled at her and pulled her closer, until their bodies nearly touched.

"I can dance, in theory." His cheeks darkened, taking on a warmer hue. "I've been taught to dance, I mean. I could … be your teacher—just for the night. Maybe?"

Her cheeks flushed with heat, and he placed a hand lightly on her waist. With his guidance, she rested her hand against his shoulder and they danced. Slow and clumsy at first, but she couldn't pull her gaze from his.

They talked about everything and nothing at all—Haven, the forest surrounding the palace, the beauty of the stars in the darkest hours of the night, her days full of training and his full of study. Time slipped past entirely unheaded while she stood in his arms.

In their shadowy corner of the ballroom, their bodies moved without thought. Anastasia surprised herself with grace, easily following where he led. Caught in the calming pool of his eyes, they danced until time ceased all together. No one else existed—only him.

CHAPTER 10

Meredith

Meredith smoothed a hand down her skirt. Alix had left to greet her father, meaning that Meredith stood alone among the glitter and dazzling lights of the palace.

Meredith simply watched and listened. All around her, the gossip of the Court of Dreams came to life. Trivial things, like marriage plans among the houses or scandals and secrets. She didn't care about such matters, but she listened all the same. Even rumors could be useful, occasionally.

A pair of ladies murmured on the edge of the dance floor. Their eyes darted about the room and they kept silk fans near their faces. Such suspicious behavior often hid the most interesting secrets. Meredith subtly drew closer to them, curiosity driving her.

She recognized them—Sanza, youngest daughter of Viscount Caine, and Liriel, the only daughter of Marquess Seai. Meredith had never liked the leering grin that Liriel often wore and was a bit surprised to see Sanza, as kind as she'd always seemed, spending time with the woman.

"The prince has been disappearing almost every day into the wooded section of the garden. Don't you think it's strange? Do you suppose he has a secret lover?" Sanza said, hiding her lips behind a silk fan. The dark purple fabric matched her dress perfectly. Her auburn hair cascaded down her back in thick, natural curls.

"Lover? Ridiculous." Liriel, dressed in deep red shimmering fabric, leaned closer, the perfectly formed curls of her black hair falling forward. "Haven't you seen those ridiculous horns? He hides them under his hooded cloak, but we all know he is more Brynian beast than Silvid. He can shift. I've seen it myself. He's probably running around the trees like a rabid dog."

Meredith's ears perked. Magic. What interesting gossip she had found. She grinned as her thoughts ran away with her. Her mother wanted her to marry the prince. She wanted magic returned to Silvis. If this was true, then her plan was painfully simple.

"You have not!" Sanza said. Her voice trembled from her effort to keep quiet.

Liriel scoffed. "I've spent most of my life in the palace. Even if I haven't seen him use magic, I know it's true."

Sanza chuckled. "You are always so funny, Lady Liriel."

Liriel snapped her black fan closed. "I'm serious. He's probably doing horrid things out there."

Meredith rolled her eyes. This was precisely why she hated the social season. She stepped forward, looking at Liriel out of the side of her eye as she walked past the two women. "If you really had seen him, I doubt you'd be talking so openly about it," she said.

Sanza pressed her fingers against her lips, likely stifling a surprised squeak, but Liriel only glared. Meredith could feel Liriel's annoyance stabbing against the back of her head as she walked away, once again scanning the ballroom for anything of note. Music played. A soft waltz floated in the air, which was cool against her bare arms.

In a shadowy corner, red and gold fabric fluttered. Meredith raised her brows at the scene she now witnessed. Anastasia and the prince of Silvis danced in a lonely corner where no one else might notice them. She should talk to the prince. She knew her mother would want her too, but as she approached, Meredith lost the will to interfere with their dance.

Laughing, Anastasia's golden eyes seemed to glow with an inner fire as she spoke with Vasileios. Though she didn't remember ever hearing Anastasia's laughter, Meredith was more surprised by the prince. He looked at Anastasia as if the sun and moon set on her smile. He hung on her words as if they held the secrets of every realm.

They spoke in hushed whispers as they moved in each other's arms to the music surrounding them, and Meredith couldn't help but overhear.

"What's it like, then?" Anastasia asked. "My flames feel like a pool of liquid gold and when I call them, it's almost ..." She bit at her lower lip, staring up into his green eyes. "Addictive. That rush of heat that could never hurt me is, sometimes, my only comfort."

Meredith turned away. She shouldn't listen. At the edge of her vision, a familiar face came into view and the tension left Meredith's shoulders almost instantly. Lady Kamiya Uviel stood at the edge of the room, watching the fae dance with a wistful expression. She was a quiet woman, nearly three centuries old, with thick bands of gray streaking her dark, fiercely curly hair that piled on top of her head with strings of glittering jewels. She wore a long gown of deep emerald green that made the rich brown of her skin seem to glow in the warm light of the ballroom.

In her hesitation, the prince's words found their way to her ears.

"Well, in some ways, it's the same for me. When I shift, I don't have to hide anymore. Sometimes, it's my only comfort too," Vasileios said in a whisper. His lips hovering near Anastasia's ear.

His words halted Meredith's steps. Liriel's claim was true. The prince was a mage who felt the weight of the Court's hatred even more than she did. Meredith hurried off. Her heart thundered against her chest. Could it be so simple? Marry the prince. Change Silvis for the better. He was obviously falling for Anastasia—a human that the queen would certainly not let him marry; if he were to marry Meredith, then she'd willingly let it be a marriage in name only. Meredith could have it all—her mother's wishes for a perfect marriage, magic, and, most importantly, Alix. But what to say? How could she pull this off? Her thoughts spiraled around her.

Meredith needed time to think about how to approach the prince. A distraction would ease her mind. There was no rush, after all. This was only the beginning of the fae social season. She'd take it slow and meticulously plot how she'd win over the prince.

Kamiya would be a perfect antidote for the mess her mind had become. Meredith made her way to the older woman's side, picking up two glasses of sparkling wine on the way.

"Lady Uviel," Meredith said. "A pleasure to see you tonight." Meredith offered one of the two glasses. Kamiya turned towards Meredith and took the glass with a warm smile.

"Good evening, Lady Meredith. I'm surprised you're bold enough to stand next to me tonight. Did your mother not attend?" Kamiya raised a brow, mischief glinting in her eyes.

"I am quite bold," Meredith said, taking a sip of her wine.

Meredith didn't care how much her mother disliked the widow; she considered Kamiya a friend, one of very few. Besides, her mother's dislike of Kamiya was ridiculous. Meredith chalked it up to jealousy—why else would she be so adamant against Meredith listening to Kamiya's stories of her mate? Her mother always said soulmates were a useless thing to aspire to and Kamiya was only filling her head with nonsense. "Mother is here, but I'd rather be here with you, no matter her thoughts."

"Ah. I see. You've missed me." Kamiya chuckled. "It has been a long time since I've seen you, little duck."

"Well," Meredith fidgeted, cheeks heating with embarrassment at the sentiment and endearment. "Of course I have ... missed you. How is the estate?" Meredith's attention wandered, straying across the ballroom until her eyes landed on Alix, who stood in conversation with her father, the General.

Alix nodded along with whatever the General was saying, which was the norm. Why didn't she think for herself? Question his decisions? Question tradition? Meredith wanted Alix at her side, but they viewed so many things differently -- especially magic. Alix would see the truth of it eventually, wouldn't she? If Meredith just showed her somehow. If only their world could be as it once was, back when the Silvid fae used their magic to build the roads and the cities, to shape the realm by their desires. Whether right or wrong, Alix always listened to authority. The prince was higher in rank than almost any other fae. If Meredith could convince the prince, then Alix would listen. She would understand.

"Empty as ever now that all my ducks have flown away. Who are you staring at with such a look?" Kamiya stepped closer, craning her head to see the line of Meredith's gaze. "Your love. But why the sour expression?"

Meredith drained her glass and sat it on a low table a few steps behind her. She was always careful to hide her feelings behind a mask, but she'd let her control slip. Her lips thinned into a line of displeasure. One of many reasons she'd despised society functions—she couldn't relax for even a moment. She shook her head slightly. "Nothing. I was just ... lost in thought, I suppose."

"Having problems?"

Meredith suppressed a scoff. When were she and Alix not having problems? That would be the better question. How fate had linked them together with the threads of a mate bond, Meredith would never understand.

Kamiya clicked her tongue. "It's not supposed to be easy, you know."

Meredith furrowed her brows. "What do you mean? We're mates."

"I know that, duck. Fate doesn't just give you your person, and that's it. There is no simple happy ever after. A soulmate is the person you're destined for, sure, a love stronger and deeper than any other..." Kamiya's eyes grew distant and glistening. "But all relationships are work. You grow with them and the relationship grows with you. Do the work to make it work."

Meredith wrapped her arms around herself, rubbing a hand up and down one arm. "But how do I do that? We fight almost every day over something." Though, if Meredith was honest with herself, that something was almost always the same things—magic and their conflicting ambitions. Meredith wanted change, something she could only do if she played the games the nobles played. Alix wanted—Meredith didn't even know what Alix wanted most days. Especially now. It just seemed like she wanted to be a perfect copy of her father—the ideal knight, the next general of the queen's forces, a honed blade bent towards protecting the realm.

"Look here, Mere," Kamiya said, brushing her fingers across Meredith's forearm in a comforting back-and-forth motion. "You choose her. Every day. Choose her and it will turn out all right. You'll figure everything else out along the way. Trust me. The late lord and I had our fair share of troubles. Being mates doesn't smooth over the bumps on the journey. Now, why don't we go get something sweet?"

"Alright." Meredith gave her a small smile. Choose Alix? She could do that. Alix still stood by the general, but when Meredith glanced at her again, Alix gave her a broad smile and tossed her a wink that made her heart flutter. She would have both Alix and her ambitions. All of her hopes relied on the prince.

CHAPTER II

Anastasia

Dancing with the prince, Anastasia spent almost the entire evening in a blur of bliss, until her father's irritated gaze landed on her. He stomped towards her and the prince, inciting a trickle of foreboding that ruined the peace Anastasia felt in the prince's arms.

"Prince," she said, breathless. "My father is walking towards us."

Reluctantly, she disentangled herself from him. If only she had a few more minutes. They barely talked. She wanted to know everything about him—his favorite food, what he liked to do in the afternoons, what he thought about her, but their time together was already ending. The thought pained her more than it should have. She'd only just met him. She frowned at her own thoughts, trying to make sense of it all.

"Anastasia," her father called. His voice was stern, clearly displeased.

The prince turned, bowing his head with respect. "Commander Creon, I am pleased to see you at court," he said.

Her father turned his attention to Vasileios, giving a curt nod. "Good evening, prince. I would like a word with my daughter, if you'll excuse us."

The prince stepped away. Losing his nearness hit Anastasia like a sudden winter breeze.

"As you desire, Commander," he said. His bright green eyes caught hers one last time. "Thank you for dancing with me," he said. "Perhaps I'll find you again on the dance floor."

Her father blew a puff of air through his nose. "I doubt that, prince. It seems your mother is looking for you." He gestured into the crowd. The queen was making a beeline towards him, with Lady Maia, Meredith, and Alix at her heels. Strange.

Anastasia wished she could listen in, curiosity and dread pooling in the pit of her stomach, but before the other fae arrived, her father had pulled her away and out into the crisp air of a courtyard.

Out in the courtyard with her father, Anastasia's eyes scanned the darkness. On the edge of the light, a broad and muscular fae man stood, wearing a strange blend of armor and formal attire. He looked to be about the queen's age, though that meant little to Anastasia, considering the fae aged differently than humans.

Anastasia squinted her eyes at him as they drew closer. He wore his muddy brown hair in a high ponytail, braiding strands away from his face, exactly like Alix. "I cannot believe you wasted almost the entire night dancing with the prince. Why did you not dance with the courtiers?" Creon asked in a tight whisper.

Anastasia blinked at him, dumbfounded. She struggled for an excuse and found herself saying, "I would think the prince would have more importance than mere courtiers. Would his words not be enough to sway his own parents?"

Her father sighed, frustrated. "The boy has nothing to do with the court, with politics, with anything. I hope you remember the sigils Shiloh taught you. The mages need help solidifying the last wall of the barrier, and then we're leaving," he said.

A few steps closer and the man waved to them both with a friendly smile and said, "Commander, good to see you again."

"General Xander, I didn't expect to see you here in the courtyard."

"It's a lovely night," General Xander said. Anastasia hovered at her father's side. This definitely was Alix's father, though Anastasia didn't think she looked much like him other than the way they both tied their hair and their eyes, which were bright blue and stood out against his skin, tanned from long hours in the sun. "Is this your daughter?" General Xander asked. "I don't believe we've ever met."

"Yes. This is Anastasia. Now, if you'll excuse us, we have some business to attend to for the queen," Creon said, taking a step away towards the shadowy edges of the courtyard.

General Xander bowed. "A pleasure to meet you, Miss Anastasia. Alix told me that you took down a nasty beast on your own. You must be quite the fighter."

Anastasia stiffened, recalling how she'd first met Alix after fighting the creature in Haven. Alix and Meredith had found her bleeding on the charred remains of the beast. She curtseyed, her breath shaking as she replied. "Thank you, General. She compliments me."

"We really must take our leave," Creon said again.

"Wait, but a moment," General Xander said, holding up his hand. "I have a question for you, Commander."

"General, is this urgent? The queen herself has set a task before me."

"My question is one from the queen as well," General Xander said. "I could walk with you, if you'd like?"

"No," Creon said with a sigh. "Anastasia, go ahead of me. I'll be right behind you. Go quickly. You'll need to go beyond the palace wall. You'll see their lights." With a hand on her back, he hurried her towards the darkness.

Anastasia nodded, giving an awkward goodbye as she disappeared into the courtyard's shadows. Once she felt confident that the general was no longer watching, she picked up the front edge of her skirt and she jogged, dragging the rest of the frilly dress behind her, uncaring of the dirt that might muddy the hem. Alone in the dark, her imagination ran wild, so she picked up her pace. She ran until she made it past the stone walls that encircled the palace and into the forest that separated the main Capital and the royal grounds.

Her unease intensified. Sparse forest surrounded her, and the shadows stretched, hiding her from even the pale starlight. Anastasia searched until she saw the subtle golden glow of Havenite magic through the trees. She ran. Her skirts caught on thorns, but she kept pushing, fleeing from her own anxiety. No matter her strength, she had barely survived her first encounter with a Hollow. She wouldn't survive alone if there was more than one. *The palace was safe.* She repeated that phrase like a mantra until she broke through the trees and into a clearing where three humans stood, wearing the red and gold robes of Haven's mages.

Two of her father's mages stood, speaking ancient spells. Shiloh was nowhere to be found. She'd hoped he would be here, a comfort to the fear that threatened to strangle her. Fire spewed from their lips with each word. Anastasia grimaced and was glad she didn't have to rely on the old ways—the spoken spells and sigils. Battle magic was intuitive. When she fought, flames roared from her fingertips and down her blade, a flurry of fire and violence. This was anything but that.

"What do you need me to do?" she asked.

A third mage stood off to the side and gestured for her to approach. "We need more flame than the environment is producing, my lady," he said.

"Don't call me that," she reminded him, and took her place near the other mages. Her fingers stretched towards the sigil on the ground. It glowed softly, like flickering candlelight. They certainly needed more than that. She couldn't imagine how tired they must be after setting one of these up in every corner and along the walls.

Anastasia still felt raw around the edges from where she'd nearly drained her soul of magic, but she knew her limits, so she exhaled and called her inner flame to the surface. This hadn't been the plan. Shiloh had taught her to use sigils for this, but now it seemed a wasted effort. Calling the flames was as easy as breathing. In a rush, her flames joined with the mages' and swirled at the center of the sigil. It would be over soon, and with any luck, she would have time to go back to the ballroom and find the prince again.

The wind shifted, bringing a familiar stench to Anastasia's nose. Rotten flesh. Her eyes jerked up and her flame died out as she searched the darkness beyond the trees. Before she could speak to warn the others, a loud crash had her whirling around. They were alone out there. No palace guards patrolled tonight on the far outskirts of the palace. The Silvids weren't fond of magic, so tonight the queen had left the security this far out to the Havenites.

An enormous shadow lurched into view, blinking red eyes at the four humans in the clearing. It was as big as a bear, but shaped like a wolf. Its fur was smoke and shadow, as if the creature was born of the space between stars, that infinite nothingness. Red light twisted down its paws, like vines, pulsing and undulating with its every step. Its gaping maw was the worst part of the monster—an unnatural row of jagged teeth that disappeared down its throat.

Anastasia pulled up the edge of her skirt and drew out her hidden dagger, heart pounding in her chest. Why would a Hollow be here?

The mages slid carefully away from the approaching beast, terror obvious in their shaky movements. Exhausted mages would be useless to her. They weren't warriors like her. Their training hadn't included offensive magic, unlike hers. A waste, she thought, but the mage's tower wouldn't allow offensive magic. They said it was too dangerous. Not knowing how to use battle magic when their lives were on the line was the real danger. She clenched her fist around her dagger.

Anastasia steeled herself as she breathed a halo of flame around her body and charged. The creature flinched away from her flames, scrambling away from her approach, but as she jumped to bring her dagger down on its eye, it met her in the air. Its snapping jaws barely missed her bare bicep and her blade sliced through nothingness. Her attack had missed.

What she wouldn't give to be armored up like Alix about now? She wouldn't waste time circling and watching like she had the first time. Anastasia slid to the creature's side and buried her dagger in its neck, her flames chasing away the shadows that licked the Hollow's flesh. It howled, flailing to get away from the fire that singed its skin and fur. She barely held on to her dagger as it tried to free itself from her grasp.

Black blood oozed from the wound, thick and reeking of long dead beasts. She jerked down, ripping the flesh of the Hollow as it whirled around on her, sinking fangs into her thigh. She shrieked in pain and her flames died out. Her magic waned. She wished she'd strapped her sword to her dress, despite what Luna had said about fae balls.

She dropped to her knees, screaming again as her flesh ripped from the jaws of the beast, and rammed her dagger into the Hollow's eye. Her own bright red blood mixed in the mud with the slimy black of the Hollow.

The creature reared back in pain. Anastasia stared at it, calculating her next move in a rush fueled by adrenaline and fear. The Hollow lunged forward, its open jaws angling for her throat. Anastasia rolled away. She tried to call the flames to her fingertips, but she felt on the edge of a dark precipice, like one step would unravel her soul and the bottom of that pit something waited to swallow her whole..

The Hollow turned on her again, prowling closer. On her hands and knees, she hastily smeared her fingers in the dirt, trying to replicate the sigil that Shiloh had taught her. "Ignite. Ignite. Ignite," she muttered to herself as she fumbled in the blood-soaked dirt.

Her fingers shook, and she stared up at the creature that would surely be her end. A flash of steel caught her eye as a heavy sword fell down onto the Hollow's neck. Its head cleaved off and hit the ground with a grotesque splat before rolling towards her.

With the beast's death, Anastasia felt her body go limp from exhaustion. She sank to the ground. It was over and she was alive.

CHAPTER 12

Meredith

After leaving Kamiya and making her rounds through the crowded ballroom to chat with the various nobles of the Dream Court, Meredith finally stood at Alix's side. General Xander had disappeared into the courtyard, claiming a need for fresh air, so they were alone. At least, as alone as they could be among the nobles twirling and laughing, scheming and schmoozing.

Alix turned, presenting one of her mischievous smiles as she pulled Meredith against her. Alix's warm touch shocked down her spine. "You'll dance with me, won't you, my love?"

Heat flushed down Meredith's neck, sending tingles across her skin. "I've been waiting all night for you to ask."

The music slowed into another waltz. Meredith had learned to dance almost immediately after she learned to walk and in moments like these, she was exceedingly glad that Alix had let her teach her how to do the court dances. Alix held her firmly—a bit too close for a waltz, really, but she wouldn't breathe a word. Meredith couldn't help but smile as she stared up into the eyes of her mate—the one person promised to her by fate.

They moved slowly, bobbing up and down in the familiar steps. They could have it all, couldn't they? Just like Kamiya said, they just had to choose each other. It would work out. It had to.

Meredith's mother and the queen made their way across the hall. Her mother's gaze fixed on Meredith, and although the Duchess laughed openly with the queen, her displeasure with her daughter was evident in the tightness of her eyes. What had she forgotten?

The prince. Sweat dappled Meredith's skin. She'd completely forgotten that her mother intended to talk to the queen tonight about arranging her marriage. Meredith needed more time. She was supposed to have more time. Were they so eager to arrange the marriage? No. The queen wouldn't decide so hastily.

Meredith took a deep breath, soothing her nerves. She told herself that Queen Harmoni was only coming to speak to her. Because of her mother's friendship with the queen, Meredith had always been close to Queen Harmoni, always underfoot. It would be a normal conversation, a polite hello, Meredith reassured herself.

As soon as the queen and her mother stopped near them, Alix broke away from their dance, bowing her head to the queen in greeting, like the good little knight she was.

The queen waved her hand. "Rise. Rise. No need for that," she said with a laugh. "Good to see you both, Alixandra, Lady Meredith. The Duchess and I would love to introduce you to Vasileios. It's his first time out in society."

"And we both think you two would be a perfect marriage match," her mother said.

"Vasil isn't particularly keen on marriage, though," the queen said with a laugh. "I'm sure he'll need some convincing, my dear."

Nervousness made her breath shake, but she nodded. Her thoughts turned to the conversation she'd overheard. Vasileios shared her suffering—the pain of isolation from magic, the weight of ridicule for what was only natural. She could take things slowly, feel it out. Speaking to him was, after all, a prerequisite for any other plans she may have. This was the first step to the future she wanted for Silvis—a future where magic lived and breathed in the Court of Dreams again.

"Of course," Meredith said. "We would love to meet the prince."

Her mother nodded, a thin smile on her lips. The queen, also smiling, led them towards a corner of the ballroom. The same corner he'd danced with Anastasia. Was she still there at his side? Or did he merely hide from the ridicule of the nobles who called him the goat prince, their fear barely hiding behind their sneers?

As they approached, Meredith saw him. He sat on the couch that lined the walls, tucked away in a shadowy nook. He was alone. His green eyes were full of some nameless sorrow that disappeared so quickly that Meredith wondered if she'd imagined the fleeting emotion on his face.

"My son," the queen said with a happy sigh. "I'd like to introduce you to some wonderful young ladies."

The prince pushed himself from the couch to stand before his mother and her company.

"This is Duchess Maia and her daughter, Lady Meredith," she said with a polite flourish of her gloved hand.

Meredith watched as her mother curtseyed, spreading her dark skirts that glittered in the light of the candelabras. Meredith mimicked her mother, curtseying with the side of her blue gown delicately held in her hands.

"And this is General Xander's daughter, Alixandra."

"Alix," Meredith corrected as Alix shot her a reprimanding glance and sharply dipped into a curtsey that made the swirling metal that laid over top her red dress clink together musically. Meredith only barely kept from rolling her eyes at Alix. The queen was her mother's best friend, so Meredith knew the queen wasn't the type to be offended by something so simple. Alix hated her full name. If she wouldn't stand up for herself in something as simple as that, Meredith had to.

Vas returned the politesse with a bow. "A pleasure to meet you," he said. His face was a calm mask, emotionless as he stood waiting for his mother to continue. Meredith wondered how many other rumors were true. The courtiers gossiped incessantly about the prince. She knew now, from his own words, that he used magic. Some of the gossip said he was a lazy, hopeless prince napping in the flowers like a wild animal. Others, the quietest voices, said he and the king consort were spies from the Brynian Court of Wild.

Meredith thought the courtiers were mostly idiots, but she knew what it felt like to have a heritage—a magic—that you couldn't practice openly. With two powerful lines of magic within him, she imagined it must be worse for him. There was no way he couldn't feel the call, that bubbling urge to do, to create, to be wild and free as fae once were.

Meredith blinked out of her thoughts. Her mother and the queen were retreating, chattering and laughing their way to the other side of the ballroom.

Alix sank down onto the couch as soon as the two women turned away and held a hand out to Meredith. She slid her fingers into Alix's palm. The small comfort of contact settled on Meredith, and she relaxed. In that moment, only Alix existed, who smiled up at her with mischief.

Meredith only had a second before Alix pulled her forward with a playful tug that sent her tumbling onto the cushion and nearly on top of Alix.

Meredith squealed and swatted at Alix, who simply laughed. Alix didn't let go of her hand as Meredith situated herself on the couch next to Alix while the prince still stood. She opened her mouth to reprimand Alix, but noticed the possessive smirk that her mate levelled at the prince. Guilt swam in Meredith's gut. Alix knew that the Duchess and the queen expected her to marry the prince. Of course Alix would make a point, showing the prince who really had Meredith's heart.

Meredith pulled her hand delicately from Alix's hand and smoothed her skirts. She couldn't let this stop her plans. Indecision twisted Meredith's stomach into knots. What should she do? If she didn't tell him her intentions now, would he do something rash—like run away with Anastasia? or make some deal with another noble desperate to climb up ranks even for a loveless marriage?

When she left the palace tonight, it may be a long time before she returned. The situation with the Hollows was too important. Suddenly, she realized that she didn't have the entire social season. All she had was tonight to convince the prince to marry her.

Alix relaxed beside her, the fiercely possessive grin never leaving her face. Meredith's heart ached. She couldn't lose this opportunity to live the life she wanted—even if it meant that Alix might not forgive her for the words she would say tonight.

With a resolve she didn't truly feel, Meredith made her decision; she would lay everything out tonight and hopefully find a way they could all have what they wanted.

"Prince," Meredith began. "I realize why my mother presented me to you, and I feel as if you and I can work through some kind of understanding."

Alix continued to glare at the prince, but he ignored her and sat down. "Okay?"

"Do you want to be married?" Meredith asked.

"Well ..." Vas said. The emotionless mask he'd been wearing fell away for a moment, once again showing the sadness beneath. "Not like this. No. I want to marry for love and that will never happen."

"Exactly," she said, nervousness making the blood rush through her ears in a thundering hum. "But we could help each other." Meredith's fingers intertwined with Alix's again. "I am completely, wholly, uninterested in marrying you."

Meredith continued. "And it's not as if my mother will let me marry a mere soldier like Alix." Alix stiffened beside her, jaw clenching. "If my marriage to you falls through, she'll find another young noble for me to marry that will better our standing or provide some gain to the house."

"Where do I fall in to all of this?" Vas asked, crossing his arms tight against his chest. Though he seemed to try his best to keep his eyes on Meredith, his gaze kept flicking to Alix with a slight frown.

"Well, that depends." Meredith tightened her fingers on Alix's hand, taking comfort in her warmth. There would be no turning back. She would need more than the lure of an open marriage to snare the prince. Any ambitions fae could offer him freedom in marriage. She would need to use their shared pain—magic.

Alix and Meredith had fought about magic before—on a more philosophical level, like if the legends were real, if magic truly corrupted, and things like that. Just thoughts, but Meredith had never revealed her desire to bring it back to Silvis. She'd never told Alix that she'd been practicing magic for years now, but tonight—at least part of that dishonesty would fall away. She just had to trust that Alix would still choose her after tonight. "I feel as if I can trust you, so I'll ask—What do you want from life? What is your greatest desire?"

"That seems like a big question," he said. His eyes searched the crowd and Meredith noticed the moment he'd found Anastasia. He had it bad. Meredith smiled, despite the nerves making her body feel weak. She remembered the first time she'd met Alix—she'd felt the same way the prince seemed to now.

"Of course it is, silly prince, but I think I know what you want. I've heard the rumors." She leaned across the couches towards him, lowering her voice. Here it was. She was taking a risk, but she didn't want to play it safe anymore. "You can shift, can't you? So it only makes sense that you'd want magic returned to Silvis, right? You are Brynian, after all—a descendant of the Wild Court, where magic flows freely. It makes sense that you'd wish for a taste of your father's homeland."

His eyes widened, gaze darting around. "What? No." He wiped his palms against his trousers. His apparent nervousness only confirmed what Meredith thought about him.

She shushed him. "There's no one else around. Be honest. Wouldn't it be better if we had magic? If the Silvids accepted their true nature, we would be as we were meant to be. Don't you want that?"

"Wait," Alix said. She tugged on Meredith's hand. "You said nothing about magic to me."

Maybe she should have talked to Alix before now, but if she had told Alix of her plan, she would have stopped her from confronting the prince, wouldn't she? Or was the prince just an excuse to tell Alix the truth? Either way, it was too late now. She wished they had the telepathic ability of bonded mates. She wished she could tell Alix they would talk later, but she couldn't share her thoughts, so instead she just patted Alix on the thigh, hoping to soothe her. Meredith was doing what she must to secure their future together, if only Alix could see that now. "Magic is in our nature, just like it is in yours, Prince. You and I could usher in a new era."

"Meredith," Alix said. Her voice wavered, sounding nervous and hurt.

"That's not possible," the prince said, shaking his head.

"It will be slow going, yes, but —" Meredith tucked a strand of hair behind her ear. She needed to convince him. She had staked all her hopes for herself, and Silvis, on this half-brynian prince. "With your help, I believe it's possible."

"I don't know," he said, sinking back into the couch, putting distance between them.

"Just think about it," she said. Now, she would put the final nail in the coffin—his obvious desire for love would surely make him see that she was the only possible marriage prospect. "We live in Haven with the humans. At the very least, it would be an excuse to see Anastasia. I saw you dancing with her earlier. Your mother would never let you marry a human, you know, but if you were to marry me, you could be with anyone you pleased."

Meredith stood and pulled Alix up with her. She could leave the prince to his thoughts. He would need time to think it over, but Meredith was confident that he would choose her. No one else would give him both magic and an uncomplicated marriage. She'd done what she set out to do—present herself as the best marriage option to the prince. Now, she just had to deal with the consequences.

The ball was nearly over. The carriage was likely waiting for them out front, so Meredith pulled Alix towards the front and out onto the lawn. Alix followed obediently, still holding onto Meredith's hand with the gentle reverence she always did. Meredith's heart twisted with guilt.

As they stood in the garden with the pale moonlight illuminating the planes of their faces, Meredith turned to look Alix in the eyes. The pain written there speared through Meredith. How could she follow her dreams of magic when her heart, standing before her personified, ached so much?

"You said nothing of bringing magic back to Silvis. I refuse to aid you in this foolishness," Alix hissed. "Absolutely not, Mere."

"It's a part of who we are! Why do you insist on denying it?" Meredith asked, leaning heavily into Alix, their hands intertwined between them. "I'm sorry," she whispered. "I should have talked to you first. The prince could be our only chance to be together. You could follow in your father's footsteps. I'll be the perfect daughter my mother wanted. And we can be together. Anyone could offer the prince an open marriage, but I can offer him knowledge of magic. It's the only way to convince him to marry me, so we can be together. If even the prince sees the value of magic, won't you, too?"

Alix turned to Meredith. She rested her hands on either side of Meredith's jaw and drew close, resting her forehead against Meredith's until their noses nearly touched.

"I don't understand your fascination with magic. I've tried to understand. I'm trying to... but," Alix whispered. "It's dangerous. I don't want to lose you. I can't lose you. I don't know if I can accept that part of you." The thread of their mate bond vibrated, feeling more fragile than it ever had before.

"Magic, and all that comes with it, is our birthright. Whatever comes, you won't lose me unless you choose to let go."

"I'll never let you go, Mere." Alix squeezed her hand and Meredith felt the truth in those words wash over her like a comforting rain.

"And neither shall I."

They would figure it out, Meredith thought. She would figure it out, somehow.

CHAPTER 13

Anastasia

The creature's head fell to the ground with a grotesque thud. It took a moment for the body to catch up, but it eventually crumpled to the ground. Its stinking blood soaked into the dirt.

Anastasia, still wreathed in flames and covered in blood and dirt, looked up to her rescuer. Her father stood with a stern expression, wiping his bloodied blade along his cloak. He looked over his shoulder at the sigil, which, miraculously, was in place and stable. Then he gestured at the mages and barked his orders.

"We're leaving. Get Lady Meredith and Bludeg. Speak nothing of this," he said. Once they left, he turned his attention back to his daughter, assessing her wounds.

He knelt on the ground beside her. With the deft fingers of a seasoned warrior, her father tended to her wounds, tying them with fabric cut from her own dress.

"This is bad," Anastasia said, wincing at the tightness of the fabric on the jagged gashes in her leg.

Her father stood, and his gaze slid along the horizon toward the palace. Safety hid behind a wall of trees and shadows. He inhaled, letting the silence sit between them for a moment. The rust smell of blood hung heavily in the air, mixing with the lingering scent of the Hollow's rotted flesh. Anastasia's stomach churned with nausea. She was glad she hadn't eaten at the ball. If she had, Anastasia knew she would vomit in the dirt at her father's feet.

"We need to get you to Lady Meredith."

"What do you mean?" she asked. He couldn't know Meredith's secret, could he? How would he? But why else would he want to rush her to Meredith's side?

"You already know what I mean, Ana. Come on, then. We're going home." Her father bent down again, sliding a hand beneath her knees and another across her back, preparing to pick her up. Anastasia stiffened. She really didn't want to be carried, but knew she couldn't walk on her own.

"Don't we need to tell the queen that a Hollow was at the perimeter?"

"I have secured a deal with the queen. She agrees that it's perfectly safe here at the palace. They don't need the soldiers, so they'll send them to us. I won't jeopardize that deal or cause hysteria among the court over one dead Hollow."

"But–" Anastasia began.

Her father stood, hoisting her up in his arms with a grunt. "That Hollow is dead. It's done. We killed it and now the barrier is in place. It was a lone Hollow."

"Why would it be all the way here?"

Her father didn't answer, and Anastasia didn't ask again. She couldn't change his mind. Before the ball, her father had told her of the meeting he'd had with the queen. She suspected something about the desert drew the Hollows to it. If there really were more Hollows heading to the desert, then Haven would need the extra blades.

The carriage waited for them far from the prying eyes of the guards stationed just outside the open doors of the palace. Anastasia heard Alix and Meredith's angry murmurs before she saw them. The two women were locked in an embrace, faces pressed close, despite the fierceness of their words. Anastasia wondered what it would be like to love someone like that, to be on the edge of love and hate—or at least, that was the way it seemed to her. In truth, she barely knew the two fae.

Creon cleared his throat as they neared. "Lady Meredith, Anastasia will need your assistance—in the carriage's privacy, of course."

The two women turned to Anastasia and took in her ragged appearance— dress ripped, muddy, bloody, and singed.

"Of course, Commander," Meredith said instantly, patting Alix on the arm as she drew away, moving to help Anastasia into the carriage.

"This isn't over, Mere," Alix said.

Meredith didn't respond as she entered the carriage after Anastasia. Lady Maia was nowhere to be found.

"Alright. Let's see it," Meredith said, shifting closer.

Anastasia turned, kneeling in the carriage, her face a breath away from the glass. She watched the palace lights as Meredith fiddled with the bandages on the back of her lef thigh, where the worst damage was. Pain jolted through her as Meredith prodded the wound.

"You need to sit still, Anastasia," Meredith whispered. "This will scar, but I believe ... it will be okay. It will be enough," she said, though Anastasia wondered who she was trying to convince? Her or herself?

Anastasia could feel the warm tingle of Meredith's magic. It seared through her flesh, and she jerked back against the cushioned bench, barely able to suppress a scream at the sudden pain. It hadn't hurt like this the first time. She panted, trying to ignore the pain and the slow relief that came with it.

"Why does my father know of your magic?" Anastasia asked through teeth gritted against her discomfort.

Meredith's head jolted up, red-ringed eyes wide. "Shhh! Keep your voice down. I healed you, and you weren't careful enough. How else would he have found out?"

"I'm sorry. My mother…"

Meredith sighed, exhaustion obvious in the set of her eyes. "I don't have the energy to navigate your apologies. Just try harder to keep your promise, yes?"

"Yes. I will, Meredith."

"Good, now be quiet, so I can focus on fixing this mess you've made." Meredith leaned closer, running her fingers over her injury. "Your flesh is so torn it could take me hours to place your nerves and muscle fibres in the right place. You're lucky that I have enough practice mending while moving blood, or you'd already be dead."

Obeying her order, Anastasia frowned and looked out the carriage window, desperate for a distraction.

A lone figure standing in the empty courtyard with his cloak billowing in the gentle wind captivated her attention. That cloak gave him away. It was the prince. Anastasia stared, subconsciously memorizing his silhouette, as the carriage jerked into motion, pulling her away from him. Her heart ached. Would she ever see him again? This silent goodbye felt too final, and she didn't understand why that thought hurt so much.

CHAPTER 14

Meredith

It was late. Well past midnight, but Meredith couldn't sleep. Instead, she sat on her bed and surrounded herself with the books that the queen had loaned her from the royal library. Meredith spent these last hours deep in the ancient myths of the Hollows. She had learned little she didn't already know, which was deeply frustrating. The books repeated the same ideas over and over again: the Hollows were a manifestation of magic and considered a curse ever since the Dae era when King Dae saved Silvis by banishing the Hollows and sealing the wellsprings.

She even found the poem about the legend of Hollows repeated multiple times. Even more frustrating than the duplicate information were the torn pages, some ripped completely out and others too damaged by time to read.. In between it all, Meredith still felt a wisp of hope as she read.

She found hints of something more—the nature of the Hollows before King Dae and what Silvis was like before the

Hollows were banished, but she only found hints—passing phrases and obscure allusions to legends she couldn't find. Every time her hope twisted to a fever pitch, she'd find a missing page or a note from the author claiming further knowledge was lost to time. Meredith couldn't find anything no matter how hard she looked. She couldn't even figure out how King Dae had sealed the wellsprings or banished the Hollows in the first place. It must have taken enormous quantities of magic to execute, but there was no trace of it.

She flipped back to the legend of Hollows poem, hoping to glean something from the ancient text, though it was little more than a nursery rhyme to scare children away from magic. She planned to move on to the books Elaine, Creon's wife, had given her after reading over the poem one more time, but before she could focus herself on the task, heavy footsteps echoed in the small, stone room that served as Meredith's bedroom in the strange little house that Creon had let her stay in while she lived in Haven.

Her head jerked up. Two sets of steps, but one was more familiar than her own heartbeat—Alix.

She waited, tapping her fingers on an open book as she stared at the doorway. Alix stepped in, relief washing across her face when she saw Meredith sitting there. Creon came in behind her, looking as irritable as ever.

Meredith held back a sigh as she stood and addressed them both. "Commander," she said. "What brings you here so late in the evening? Do you have more reading material for me?"

Creon blinked, looking taken aback by the question, then shook his head. "No. Elaine has given you everything possibly relevant, though I doubt our histories will be of any help."

Meredith was inclined to agree with him there, but she wouldn't abandon all hope. Not yet.

"No," he repeated. "You're needed on patrol."

"Patrol?"

"Scouts sighted a few Hollows just an hour ago. Are you not here to investigate the creatures?"

Meredith's breath caught in her throat. More Hollows existed. She would still have a chance to see them. Her lips curved in an involuntary smile. "Of course. I'll get ready quickly." She turned and began scrambling about the room for her armor, which she rarely wore. She pulled a pair of chainmail leggings over her pants, fastening them in place at her hips. She picked up her leather bodice, admiring the metal working that swirled across it like lace—more beautiful than protective, she'd always thought.

"Anastasia is already waiting in the Western temple. I trust you can both find your way," Creon said.

"Yes, commander," Alix said, lifting her chin as she straightened up by the door.

"Then, I'll leave you to it." Creon glanced at them both, nodded, and then walked out of the room, retreating into the blue dim of Haven.

Without words, Alix helped Meredith with her armor, pulling the straps tight and straightening her belts. Meredith fastened her rapier to her side, then hesitated for a moment. She wasn't quite used to the weight of the axe yet. It had been her father's, which he'd passed down to her, but a rapier wouldn't do much if a Hollow came after her.

She pursed her lips. These were the creatures from the ancient legends. Could she really wield a weapon against them? Seconds ticked by. Alix stood beside her, waiting with a watchful curiosity. Moments like these, Meredith swore their bond had clicked in place. In that thick silence, it was almost like Alix could read her thoughts and emotions.

Meredith reached for the axe, but left the cover across the blades, and fastened it across her back. She wouldn't be a fool. No matter how beautiful a wolf may be, they were still predators, and the same applied to the Hollows. Though, she desperately wished it would never come to a fight against them.

Finally ready, Alix and Meredith left the house and made their way to the grand elevator of Haven that led to the Western temple. The elevator was water powered—some leftover magic by the ancient Silvids—but stairs wound, spiralling like snakes, around the side of the glass column that made up the elevator's shaft.

They stepped inside and Meredith flicked a lever, rocketing them upwards and into a tiny room in the sandstone temple. Meredith's stomach flipped. Maybe she should insist on the stairs next time. Within the elevator, there were two exits: one with an enormous door that seemed to lead outside and a second that was much smaller. Remembering the smaller door from their entry into Haven, Meredith pushed it open.

The room was small. The floor was empty except for a hatch that Meredith could only assume led to the stair case that wound around the elevator they'd just taken.

Just as Creon said, Anastasia sat on the floor in that little room, waiting for them. She looked lost in a daydream—eyes staring empty at the middle distant and a slight smile curving her lips.

"Anastasia?" Alix asked.

She blinked out of her reverie, cheeks flushing a soft pink. "Right, let's go then. The scouts saw the Hollows circling across the desert, heading towards the wellspring, so we should check there first." She glanced between the two women. "Just long sleeved tunics and armor? Do you want some gloves, hoods, cloaks? We have extra. The desert is freezing after sunset."

Before Alix or Meredith could even respond, Anastasia pushed herself off the floor and walked out of the room. She returned almost as quickly, pushing fleecy clothes into their arms. "That should do you," she said. "Get that on, and come on." Once again, she left.

Meredith furrowed her brow at the strange behavior, while Alix just laughed and began pulling on the fleeces as she moved to follow Anastasia. Hearing her mirth, Meredith couldn't help but smile. The sound sank into her bones, warming her more than the fleece ever could. Meredith tossed the cloak around her shoulders and pulled on the gloves.

Anastasia led them through the glowing halls of the temple. As she went, Anastasia brushed her fingers along the wall. Flames sparked to life at her fingertips and the fire sank into the walls, swirling around ornate patterns and racing along crevices, lighting their way. Finally, they broke into an enormous, empty room. It looked like a sanctuary. Worn grooves marked the floor, where, Meredith imagined, the faithful had once knelt in meditation or prayer. Did the humans worship the Celestial Court, like some fae did? Or was there some human divine being?

As her thoughts looped, they continued their journey through the room, and through a much smaller entryway, lined with statues. Beyond the entryway, enormous wooden doors stood open, letting the icy winds of the desert rush through and bite at their exposed faces. Meredith was suddenly very glad for Anastasia's concern and the cloak she'd given them both.

Without hesitation, they stepped out into the desert. Tonight, Meredith thought excitedly, she would see a living Hollow.

CHAPTER 15

Anastasia

They walked in silence. Only the sharp winds from the distant Abyssal Bay broke the quiet as the biting breeze rushed across the dunes. The patrol route was familiar to Anastasia—down the temple path, through the dunes, along the winding stone road, and around the wellspring. Her feet moved without conscious thought, leaving her mind to wander like it had ever since the ball at the palace.

Prince Vasileios plagued her thoughts in a way no one had before. She wondered what his favorite foods were, what he hated, what he thought about when the world was quiet. Her father had said he wasn't part of the court—why? Wasn't he the prince? Wouldn't he become the next king one day? His features blurred in her mind, only those bright green eyes standing out in her memory. Despite being unable to remember exactly what he looked like, she knew he was handsome. Perhaps that caused the courtiers' distance from him—jealousy? Who wouldn't be jealous of a prince?

She pulled her cloak tighter around her face as a gust of wind threatened to yank her hood off her head. Was he as alone as she was? Her heart clenched with sympathy — with the thought of a shared pain. As a prince, his life must be like hers, she thought, full of duty and obligation, but did he love his people the way she did? Did he not care? Was he burdened by his family's expectations? Her thoughts continued to circle back to him. No matter how much she tried to focus on the dark of the desert or the dry, earthy scent of the sand, all she could think about was him. Her Prince.

Her cheeks heated, embarrassed by her own strange fixation. Is this what being interested in a boy felt like? She'd always wanted to be loved, to love someone, but she'd never had time before, still didn't have the time to entertain such nonsense. Anastasia wasn't like the women in the knighthood, who fantasized about nights spent with men they didn't even know. The way they talked about them, about their bodies, grossed her out, if she was honest, so she'd just never bothered with dating.

She clenched her fists against her sides. It didn't matter. She closed her eyes and took a deep breath of the icy wind. She had more important things to think about other than a kind, awkward fae prince. She smiled despite herself at the memory of their meeting—his fumbling words, dancing together, laughing. Forgetting for a little while who they were supposed to be in this world and the roles they played. But that was over now. The sharp wind reminded her of that. Here in the desert, she was a knight again.

Anastasia glanced over her shoulder at the two women she'd brought out into the desert. They followed along obediently, eyes sweeping the sand. Meredith, tall and thin with her short black hair poking out of her hood, seemed almost giddy as she kept pace and searched the shadows. Alix wore a serious expression and her hand never left the hilt of her sword.

"We likely won't see anything tonight," Anastasia said, slowing her steps to walk beside them.

"But the scouts..." Meredith frowned.

"That was hours ago. You said the Hollows don't like the sun, right?"

"Yes. That's what the legends say."

"Dawn isn't far away. What few the scouts saw are likely deep underground by now. At best, I'm taking you out to see tracks of some sort that we can follow in the morning." Her heels thudded softly against the sandstone path that cut through the dunes. Each strike punctuating the silence that descended upon the group.

Alix relaxed, exhaling slowly as her fingers finally released their grip on her sword. Meredith crossed her arms, but kept her gaze out on the desert. Anastasia felt like an outsider, and she hated that. She always felt so isolated from other people. She picked at a loose thread on one of her gloves. Her father thought it best she trained separately from the other knights.

She didn't have time to make friends outside of work. She didn't even spend time with her family—they didn't have time for her either. Running the city was a heavy burden. Her role as the Keeper of Light, the one chosen by the flame of Haven, and daughter of the Haven leaders, kept her distant. She didn't want to keep that distance anymore.

"So, you two lived in the Capital?" Anastasia asked, still nervously fiddling with the loose string on her glove. Between thoughts about the prince and her own isolation, she felt restless.

"Yes," they both said in unison, pulling a smile and a sideways glance from them both. Anastasia smiled in response, feeling the warmth of their fondness for each other melt away her nervousness.

"Not always, though," Meredith said. "I'm from Kaesy on the East side of Silvis, but since my mother is so close to the queen, we spend most of our days in the Capital."

Other than the recent trip to the Capital, Anastasia had never seen other places. She wondered what Kaesy was like. Her father always said understanding of geography could make or break a battle, so she'd seen maps and read descriptions of nearly every part of Silvis during her education.

"I've always lived there. My father is the general and, though he never expected it of me, I always wanted to follow in his footsteps as a knight, so," Alix shrugged.

"And so, my Alix lives and breathes for the knighthood just like her daddy, whom she adores so much," Meredith said with a playful roll of her eyes. Anastasia didn't blame her. Though she'd barely met him, General Xander seemed like a good man. He'd been kind to her, at least.

Alix bumped her shoulder into Meredith's and the two stumbled side to side as they grappled, laughing as they tried to walk and fend off the other's advances at the same time. The melancholy returned like a wave of daggers, reminding Anastasia of how alone she was in the world. She wished she could return to the night of the ball. If she sent a letter to the prince, would he write one back? The thought made her heart flutter for a moment, before Alix and Meredith's playful scuffle brought her back to her cold reality.

"You seem pretty close," Anastasia said, dodging out of the way of Alix's heavy steps as Meredith spun her away like a dancer at the fae ball.

The two laughed, and Alix straightened herself before pulling Meredith's cloak tighter around her face. "Well, we have known each other for quite a long time. Do you remember, Mere?"

"Of course, I do. It's hard to forget a gangly teenage wannabe knight being pummeled in the courtyard for hours. I still don't know why you didn't just give up. Your father had you beaten a hundred times." Anastasia could imagine it—Alix, red-faced and bruised, wielding a sword against

General Xander's patient hand and failing repeatedly, but unwilling to yield.

Alix scoffed. "Gangly. At least I wasn't sitting around doing nothing like some little grump."

"Grump! I was not!"

Alix laughed and snatched up Meredith's gloved hand. "Sour faced little imp," Alix said, laughing as she pressed a kiss to the back of Meredith's hand.

Anastasia watched, once again feeling like she was intruding on their moment. She turned away, her stomach turning at the sudden swing of her thoughts back to the prince. An embarrassed flush crept up her neck, burning her cheeks. What would it be like to laugh with the prince again? To have his lips against her fingers?

Meredith swatted at Alix, her hand hitting her arm with a solid thud. "I apologize on behalf of Alix," Meredith said. "It's incredibly impolite of us to show affection like this, especially when we're supposed to be focused on the patrol." Meredith spoke the last words through her teeth, pointedly towards Alix.

"I get caught up," Alix said, giving Anastasia a lopsided grin. "It's difficult to resist my mate."

"Mate?" Anastasia had never heard that word before, at least not when referencing another person. "Is that what the fae call their partners? Even though Haven is part of Silvis, we don't actually have many fae visitors."

"No, not exactly," Alix said.

"It's magic," Meredith whispered. The giddy glimmer returned to her face — the same expression she'd had when they first began their patrol.

"It is *not magic*," Alix said. "A mate bond is sacred, a blessing from the Celestials. Your mate is the person who fate has chosen for you. Our souls are bound for all eternity. Even when we die and become stars in the Celestial Court, we will shine side-by-side."

"Well, yes," Meredith said. "But isn't that a kind of magic too? Celestial Court magic?"

Alix frowned. "Fine," she said. "Our legends only claim Silvid magic corrupts, so I suppose you could be right."

"That's so romantic," Anastasia said. Did she have a mate? Did fate choose someone for her? For a half-second, she dreamt perhaps she had a mate and perhaps it was the prince. Her prince. But, no. That was only a dream. Mates certainly weren't for humans like her. Fate and the Celestial Court were for the fae—part of their beliefs and customs. So, she forced her thoughts away from the green eyes of the prince that swam in her mind.

Instead, she continued down the path with Alix and Meredith, enjoying the idle chatter and learning about the lives that they had lived on the mainland of Silvis. A few steps ahead, she glanced back at them with a smile.

With Alix and Meredith by her side, talking and laughing, she didn't feel so alone. Her heart sank as she remembered this was temporary. Soon, Alix and Meredith would return to the mainland and she would be alone again. Like Shiloh, they had jobs to do, roles to fulfill. She had her own part to play in the world. She knew that, but it didn't stop the ache in the realization that she would miss them.

CHAPTER 16

Meredith

The three of them walked for what felt like hours, falling quiet when the cold became too much for their exposed faces. The thick scarves muffled their words, so they'd chosen to lapse back into the watchful silence of their patrol. Meredith couldn't remember the last time she'd ever gone on a patrol. She was technically part of the knighthood, but as a noble, things were different for her. She wasn't even high in the chain of command, but she chose what missions she went out on. In fact, most of the time, she barely participated. The rest of the knighthood thought of her as a false knight, but they didn't mind her presence. They understood. She would follow Alix anywhere and the knighthood was just one of the many places she'd followed her mate.

With each step, they drew nearer to a faint blue glow that barely cut the thickness of the night. The dunes levelled out, revealing a strange, stony plain, like a grassless meadow. In the center of the plain, the desert dropped away, revealing an enormous hole—the source of the gentle blue light. Anastasia led them closer, taking a well-worn path to the edge of the pit, where a set of stone stairs cut into the side of the hole. Pausing at the top of the stairs, they looked down.

The wellspring sat below—-a pool of clear blue liquid that glowed like the fog between stars condensed and given life. Long ago, Meredith learned wellsprings were pools of raw magic, but she'd never seen one before. The sight filled her with awe. Pulses of power radiated from the wellspring, reverberating through her bones like a siren's call—beautifully intoxicating. The edges of her vision tinged red as the magic filled her. She took a deep breath, attempting to regulate herself, hoping the red rings that appeared in her eyes when she used magic weren't surfacing in the onslaught of power from the wellspring.

The distance to the pool was as tall as the buildings in Haven. If Meredith fell into the pit, the drop would be fatal. The stairs, cut into the stone wall of the pit, wound around the wellspring in a spiral. Meredith's heart raced. Hollows. At the bottom, drinking from the magic pool of the wellspring, a handful of dark shapes became silhouettes against the soft glow of the liquid magic.

The Hollows chittered amongst themselves. She strained her ears to listen. It almost sounded like speech. The gravelly tones broke and stretched in familiar ways. Curiosity and hope spiked in her gut, only to be dashed as she noticed that Anastasia and Alix were already stalking down the stairs with their swords drawn. She rushed after them. She had to stop them, but calling out would startle the Hollows. Stones slipped beneath her feet and she went sliding down the stairs.

The noise caught the attention of the Hollows below. They lifted their jaws and screeched. The sound pierced through the air and felt like a dagger through Meredith's ears. Laying on the ground, she grabbed her head to block out the noise. Red sparks of magic leapt from her fingers in unruly bursts that soothed the pain in her head.

She pushed to her hands and knees, steadying herself on the cold stone. All she could do was watch as the Hollows bounded up the stairs, meeting the two knights that hurled towards them with flashing blades. No. No. Meredith wanted to scream, but couldn't find her voice. They hadn't attacked until she'd startled them. Maybe there was hope they could coexist. Maybe they could communicate. Nothing in the books had indicated the Hollows were anything more than wild animals born of magic, but she was almost certain they were talking to each other. Almost. If Anastasia and Alix had just waited, she could have been sure. If they just stopped.

But they didn't.

The Hollows met the cold steel of the knight's blade. Black blood fell in clotted chunks, splashing across the sand. The coppery, rotten tang filled the air, leaving Meredith nauseous. Why couldn't she get up? Why couldn't she move? The screech from the Hollow had done something to her. It drove straight to the very core of her being and rattled something loose, something she didn't think she could control. It was almost as if she could feel, could understand, the Hollow in that moment. She squeezed her eyes shut, grappling with the strange otherness inside her mind.

The fight below her was over almost as soon as it started and Alix was by her side, fussing over her crouched form.

"Mere? Mere. Are you okay? Are you hurt? We need to get you back to Haven."

Meredith felt herself being lifted. She wanted to protest, but her lips wouldn't move. She had to talk to the queen. This wasn't right, was it? Killing these creatures? She shuddered in Alix's arms, which tightened around her, as she drifted off into a dreamless sleep with only the echoes of that feral feeling the Hollow's screech had left in her heart.

CHAPTER 17

Alix

Alix saw Meredith fall, but she had been too far away to do anything. Then the Hollows attacked, and she couldn't get to her. The sight of Mere, crouched on the stairs as the red lightning of Hollow magic sparked around her, nearly stopped Alix's heart. The moment Mere had fallen unconscious, the magic had faded, but that didn't stop the panic and bile that rose in Alix's throat.

"What's happening to her?" Anastasia asked, jogging alongside her as they took the path back to Haven. The wind whipped around them, but no amount of cold air could clear the rotten stench of the Hollows from Alix's nose. She hated them. She hated magic. *This* is exactly why she'd fought with Meredith about the Hollows and magic. The infuriating woman was too complacent, too curious for her own good. But could she ever force Meredith to choose between her and the magic? Alix already knew the answer and didn't want to face the truth. *She would follow Meredith to hell and back, if only to remain at her side.*

Alix had no clue what was happening to Meredith, but she could feel something in the thread of their mate bond. Something had changed, and a trickle of Meredith's emotions dripped down the thread—sorrow, such sorrow. Overwhelming grief.

Alix's eyes burned. "I don't know," she said, holding Meredith tighter against her chest. "We should report to the queen. Those things were drinking from the wellspring—they were drinking pure magic. That must be what is drawing the Hollows to the desert." She looked down at Meredith's face. Her dark brows, standing out against the pale fawn of her skin, finally relaxed.

Nothing would stop her from leaving tonight. Whatever had happened to Meredith, the queen surely would know. She had to.

CHAPTER 18

Meredith

Meredith woke with a start to the creaking of carriage wheels. Her mind felt fuzzy and strangely fractured. She took a deep breath, recalling what had happened before she'd lost consciousness. She didn't feel the burgeoning wildness pressing at her mind any longer, and when she cracked open her eyelids, the red haze that had clouded her vision was gone. Her body felt tight. She curled on her side on the carriage bench.

Meredith's head rested in Alix's lap and an arm wrapped around her, holding her tight to smooth any bumps they may have hit. Warmth suffused her, and she shifted closer to Alix. Despite their disagreements, Alix loved her and she loved Alix. She wanted to close her eyes again and drift back to sleep. Exhaustion weighed on her body, as if she'd not just spent so much time deep in sleep.

But her movement had alerted not only Alix, but Anastasia, who sat on the bench across from them, with a history book in her hands. It was one the queen had lent Meredith.

"Mere?" Alix whispered, brushing a hand through Meredith's hair.

"Her eyes were open just a moment ago. I'm certain of it," Anastasia said.

Reluctantly, Meredith opened her eyes again and tilted her head to look up at Alix.

"Thank Celestials," Alix said, pressing her fingers into Meredith's hair again. "Are you okay? Are you hurt?"

"I'm perfectly fine, my love," Meredith said, not wanting to admit to the deep-seated exhaustion or the cramped feeling in her limbs, as if her skin stretched across bones much bigger than before. She imagined shedding skin like a snake would feel amazing. Meredith shuddered at the grotesque image her mind had created. "Where are we?"

"We're almost to the palace," Anastasia said, peeking through the curtained window beside her. She dropped the red and gold curtain and it fluttered back into place.

The palace. Meredith struggled to sit up, groaning as her muscles hesitated to move. The queen. She needed to talk to the queen about the Hollows. After watching them by the wellspring, Meredith felt certain that they could coexist somehow. She hadn't found evidence in the old texts yet, but she knew that the Hollows and Silvids had existed side-by-side for centuries before King Dae sealed the wellsprings away.

Alix brushed her hand in circles on Meredith's back, comforting her and bringing her back to the moment. "Alix," Meredith said, turning to face her. She didn't want to hide her thoughts or intentions from her anymore. Her first step had been at the ball, but she had to keep choosing Alix and choosing to be honest with her, so Meredith continued with a shaky breath. "I know you don't agree with me, but I think we can live alongside the Hollows. I need to talk to the queen about this."

Alix frowned and then tilted her head back for a moment to sigh softly at the ceiling. "I know," she said, catching Meredith's eye once more. "I don't understand it, but I could... feel your grief for those Hollows we killed."

Feel? Meredith's heart leapt. Their bond. Alix had never felt her emotions before. This had to be a good sign. She smiled and grabbed Alix's hand, squeezing gently.

"I admit you're more of a scholar than I am. I could be wrong about the beasts, but..." Alix twisted her lips back and forth and shook her head. "If you're wrong, then the Hollows will only bring death and I can't take that risk — I can't risk losing you to the jaws of a monster for your strange compassion. I won't agree with you in front of the queen, nor will I help you convince her. I can't, but I won't try to keep you from asking. If the queen agrees with you, then I have no choice but to follow orders."

"That's all I can ask," Meredith said. Her heart felt light, full of hope.

***

Hours passed like minutes, and soon they all stood in the queen's quarters—a series of maze-like rooms full of plush velvet furniture. The King Consort stood by the queen with one of their advisors and a servant with long black hair, who arranged a small round table with refreshments. Creon had sent Anastasia in his place for this report, so it was only the three of them standing before the queen.

"Your report?" The queen asked as she sat down in a fluffy armchair.

Alix stood with her arms loosely clasped behind her back. "I believe we've uncovered what has been drawing the Hollows to the desert. On patrol, we found a large group of them drinking from the wellspring. We destroyed all of them, but during the fray, something strange happened to Lady Kaesy."

Alix hesitated, and the queen tapped her index finger against her bottom lip with a perplexed expression before gesturing for Alix to continue. "After falling down the stone stairs, one beast screeched, overcoming the lady with ... magic.

Red sparks of magic. She fainted and only regained consciousness a few hours ago."

The queen crossed one leg over the other and looked between Alix and Meredith with furrowed brows. "Meredith, how are you feeling?"

"I'm feeling fine, normal, my queen."

The queen leaned forward, placing her elbow on the arm of the chair and her chin in her hand. "The wellspring is pure magic, the condensed essence of the Faerie realms. For it to be the draw of the creatures is logical, but where are the Hollows coming from in the first place?" The queen's eyes shifted to Meredith again with a raised brow.

"I'm not sure, but with more time, I may find out. I'm still reading through the books you've sent me and Lady Elaine of Haven has shown me several texts from Haven's libraries that seem promising. The humans have their own legends that have similarities with our own, though they call the Hollows by another name." Meredith stepped forward in front of Alix. "My Queen, I believe that there is more to the Hollows than we may realize. I think it's possible for us to coexist with them."

The queen cast her gaze to the ground and shook her head slowly once. "No." She placed her hand against her mouth momentarily before letting it fall away as she looked back to Meredith.

"The histories and the legends of our ancestors all say the same thing, Meredith. Magic is the source of our corruption and the great pain of the Silvid Court. The accounts from Dae, the First King, make it quite clear that there could be no court where the Hollows survive. The wellspring should have never been uncovered. That's when this all began, it seems." The queen looked at her husband. "Who sanctioned that dig in the first place?"

"I did," the King said, mirroring her frown. "Though I had no idea what they were uncovering. The Academy's project seemed innocent. Their research suggested the site to be a likely location for the Dragon's Library."

"Then the solution is clear," the queen said. "We must seal the wellspring again and exterminate any Hollows before more are born from the wellspring's influence."

"But, my queen, King Dae's seal is the only way to accomplish that goal," Meredith said.

The queen nodded and tapped her finger against her lips. "Have you come across the text of the sealing ritual?"

"No, my Queen," Meredith said. "But," she quickly added. "If given more time, I might find it."

"There is no time when our people are at risk," the queen said. "Since the ritual is still lost to time, we'll need to be creative." The queen glanced over her shoulder at the advisor standing just behind her. "Athan, you spoke yesterday of an invention by the Academy. Remind me again, please."

The man stepped forward, his dark gaze on the floor as he bowed his head. "Of course, my queen. The Academy has recently discovered a mixture that explodes when exposed to open flame. They haven't yet tested it thoroughly or in high quantities."

"Send for the headteacher. I believe this is the perfect opportunity for them to test their newest invention." Queen Harmoni relaxed back into her chair, studying Meredith's melancholy expression.

"Of course, my queen," Athan said, stepping back to his original position along the wall of the room.

"If only you'd give me a bit more time—" Meredith began, but the queen shook her head.

"No. I'm sorry," the queen said with a sad smile. "I wish I could give you more time. These legends have always been an interest of yours, and I want you to be right, but all evidence shows you are merely an idealist, my dear. Even with my fondness for you, I cannot indulge you this time."

Meredith stepped back, dropping her gaze to the floor. The queen had always understood her, always supported her.

"Bludeg," the queen said.

"Yes, My Queen," Alix said.

"I need you three to head back to Haven and begin preparations. I expect you will need warriors on standby in case our efforts at the wellspring draw out the beasts. Once matters are settled with the Academy, I'll send a company of knights to

Haven with everything needed to collapse that horrid well-spring and return it to the desert sands. You are dismissed."

The queen stood, ushering them all out of the room.

Meredith felt defeated, and she barely registered as Alix led her back to the carriage and they began their journey back to Haven. She grabbed the book Anastasia had abandoned on the carriage bench and began reading.

Hours passed as Meredith read *The Histories of King Dae and the Dawn of the Silvid Court.* The only thing Meredith found of interest was the torn remnants of a missing page. Another dead end. Everywhere she turned, everything she read, it was all a dead end. So close to the truth, but proximity didn't matter. She couldn't save the Hollows or the wellspring with wishes or her intuition.

She tightened her fingers on the leather cover and desperately hoped that the books from Haven's libraries might show her something to convince the queen, but in her heart, she feared the worst.

CHAPTER 19

Anastasia

Nearly a week had passed before the knights from the Capital arrived. Now that they were here, plans hurried along. Anastasia followed around General Xander and Alix as they made the final preparations. The entire company—knights, alchemists, Haven knights, Alix, Meredith, and Anastasia—stood at the foot of the grand entrance that led to the Western Temple in the desert above.

Despite the risk of Hollows appearing, they decided to leave at sunset. The daytime sun was too much for them to handle in full armor, but despite Meredith's reassurances that the Hollows would only come out at night, General Xander did not want to risk going out in the day without armor. Haven's mages couldn't possibly enchant enough desert armor to outfit the company of knights the queen had sent. There just wasn't enough time.

Anastasia had barely seen Meredith this week. Ever since they'd returned from the Capital, she had holed herself up in her room or the library to read. But, now that the time had come for the queen's plan, the three of them were together again. Meredith, with heavy lids and bags under her eyes, slumped as she walked a few paces behind Alix and General Xander.

"Are you feeling ill?" Anastasia asked.

Meredith shook her head, but otherwise didn't speak. She seemed resigned, broken, and exhausted.

The materials were prepared. Two alchemists from the Academy had arrived with the knights, and they stood next to a cart laden with boxes, which would be pulled by one of Haven's few horses. The entrance, which had always baffled and fascinated Anastasia, was an enormous water-powered elevator with a spiraling stone staircase wrapped around the cylinder of the elevator. The alchemists and their cart were the first to go up, loaded on the elevator and sent on, while the knights began their ascent on the stairs.

The journey was quick, much quicker than it had felt the night of the patrol. Soon the entire party was at the entrance to the wellspring, with the last warm touches of dusk finally gone. With the help of the alchemists, the knights placed the explosive charges in the walls lining the wellspring.

Anastasia watched as an uneasiness creeped up her spine. A moonless night unfolded, and one by one, stars began to twinkle, their distant light barely piercing the inky blackness above. It seemed Alix felt the same anxiety. She paced back and forth, eyes sweeping the desert horizon, while Meredith simply watched with vacant eyes.

"The explosives are in place," General Xander said, gesturing to the string on the ground by the wellspring's lip—the fuse, one alchemist had called it. "If you would, Keeper."

Now it was her turn. She recalled her lessons with Shiloh. Extending the enclosing circle of the ignition sigil into a line would allow her to ignite the sigil from a distance. Anastasia stepped forward, taking a deep breath. She crouched on the ground by the fuse and began drawing in the sand, muttering the words that Shiloh taught her. Thin golden lines of magic pooled in the symbols she drew. It felt strange—this kind of magic. She was used to battle magic, the kind that drew the flame from her very soul and being. But this? It felt empty. Shiloh had explained it, how this magic drew from the energy of the world instead, but she didn't like it. She missed the warmth she felt when she used her flames.

"Everyone, you need to be behind the line," called out General Xander. Alix began ushering the knights backwards. The noise of their retreat faded, leaving Anastasia feeling exposed. She was alone, while the rest of them were several thousand feet back, hiding behind sloping sands.

Anastasia shivered, but forced herself to stand. She walked backwards, heading towards the General and the others, muttering the spell words the entire way. The gold magic that pooled in the sigil followed her, leaving a softly glowing line in the sand. Once she'd finally joined the others, she stopped and stood by the now lengthened fuse.

"Ready?" General Xander asked with a smile that seemed intended to comfort her, to soothe her frazzling nerves.

The uneasiness heightened, but she nodded and held her hand out towards the fuse. "Yes, sir. All clear?!"

The knights scrambled back, putting even more distance between themselves and the fuse at Anastasia's feet.

"All clear," said a chorus of voices.

Anastasia called the flame to her fingertips, and it flickered, mirroring her nerves. She was as far from the wellspring as she could be. The sigil would do its job. They would be safe from the blast, but another thought nagged at the back of her mind. What about the Hollows? Where were the Hollows?

With a jerk of her hand, Anastasia dropped the flame to the ground. It raced along the golden line and in the distance, she could see as it flared around the sigil and lit the alchemists' fuse. Moments passed, and she wondered if it had worked, but suddenly the ground shook. Anastasia fell to the ground, covering her ears at the sudden onslaught of sound and wind and dust. She squeezed her eyes shut against the flurry of sand. When she opened her eyes again, her breath caught in her throat.

The wellspring still stood, unchanged, except for a shimmering light that surrounded it like a dome of magic. Remnants of flame licked the sides of the dome, but otherwise, the wellspring was entirely intact. The queen's plan hadn't worked.

Meredith laughed as she moved to stand beside Anastasia, a dry broken sound of relief. "It didn't work," she said.

"General," said a panicked voice to Anastasia's left. "There's something on the horizon."

Anastasia turned. Her stomach churned at the sight—in the distance, the sand exploded as Hollows clawed from whatever holes they slept in during the day. The beasts gathered together, racing towards them in an undulating mass of shadows. Their unnatural, garbled howls filled the night air.

"The Hollows are coming. Haven Knights — those with flames, call the fire to you!" Anastasia shouted. She'd only fought the Hollows twice, but both times, her flames had been the only thing keeping her from death. Those beasts didn't relent.

"No..." Meredith watched in horror as the horde grew near. "We need to retreat. General? Please, give the order. There's no need for this. We should retreat."

General Xander looked from the knights to the distant Hollows. "Our orders from the queen were clear. Destroy the wellspring and exterminate the Hollows." He shook his head and turned to the knights. "Prepare yourselves! Tonight, we fight."

The knights lifted their swords in response.

"Move them to the stone plateau. It will be easier to fight there instead of in the sands," Alix said to the General, who nodded and called out the order for the knights to move.

The company was only about fifty warriors, plus the two alchemists and the three of them.

When the Hollows, snarling with saliva dripping from their jagged jaws, finally arrived, the knights were ready. Anastasia was ready. Alix stood by her father at the front. Despite her obvious despair at the order to fight, Meredith stood at Alix's side.

CHAPTER 20

Alix

The Hollow's onslaught was sudden and overwhelming. Their reeking stench permeated the desert. Alix struggled to breathe as she twisted, bringing her sword down on the shadowy flesh of beast after beast. Her father, General Xander, fought beside her. His blade singing through flesh with each powerful swipe. Blood splattered his face. Alix felt strange seeing him like this—seeing the good-natured smile completely absent and replaced with a furious sneer.

The human Anastasia held her own against the Hollows. Her flames were a marvel that the beasts cowered away from moments before it consumed them. With the flick of her hand, her flames leapt down her sword. The girl was a brute, digging her flaming blade into every vulnerable space the Hollows exposed — eyes, throat, bellies. Alix watched as the human, the Keeper of Light, shoved her hand down a Hollow's throat and lit it on fire from within.

Alix couldn't draw her eyes from the flames. Humans didn't naturally have magic, so she felt certain their flames were a divine blessing because human magic was nothing like Silvid magic. Their fire warmed and saved. It was the anti-thesis of the shadowy beasts they now fought. Silvid magic could only corrupt. It birthed the Hollows. She was glad the humans brought their gift to be the light against the Hollows darkness.

Snapping jaws brought her back to the reality in front of her. Alix's attention was divided, something she couldn't afford in this struggle. Though she'd been training her entire life, Alix had never been in a fight like this. Silvis was peaceful. At least, it had been, until these disgusting creatures came out of hiding. A Hollow leapt from the swarming pack towards her, and Alix kicked out, slamming her boot into the monster's chest, pinning it to the ground as she hacked through its neck. She left it twitching, slipping quickly into death, as her eyes sought distraction once again — Meredith.

Meredith moved like a dancer, wielding her father's axe like a merciful executioner. She didn't hesitate, but she didn't needlessly strike, either. Each blow Meredith dealt brought death to the snarling beasts before her. Caught in worry and awe of Meredith, Alix didn't see the Hollow until it was too late.

The beast crept behind her and leapt for her throat. Meredith's eyes went wide as she called out with desperation. Red eyes locked to Alix's own blue. She knew then it was over. It was too late. She lifted her blade, but her heart had already succumbed to death. When her father slid between her and the beast, Alix screamed. Her throat felt raw as she threw herself forward, reaching for the Hollow as it collided with her father.

Its gaping jaws clenched around his throat, tearing flesh even as the general's blade sank deep into its heart. Alix grasped air as the two—her beloved father and the beast she hated—fell to the dust with a sickening thump that would echo in her ears for years after. Blood mixed and pooled on the sand, making black-brown mud of the desert. Terror filled Alix's bones, and she dug her fingers into the soft flesh of the Hollow, yanking the beast away. With each desperate attempt, the creature's rotting flesh and fur came away in her hands. She dug deeper, getting gore beneath her nails. Tears blurred her vision.

Meredith dropped to her side, and together, they pulled the beast away from the general. His blue eyes dulled and a soft sigh slid past his lips. "Alixandra," he whispered. His voice gurgled with blood.

"I can fix this!" Meredith said. Her voice pitched higher as red light danced between her fingertips. "Alix, let me fix this."

Magic. Meredith held magic in her hands. Her father lay dying in the dirt in front of her. Is this what it meant to have magic in Silvis? To fight, to die, to heal, to live? Could Silvid magic really heal? She'd never believed the stories of ancient healers, but Meredith hadn't lied about the Hollows. Those legends had turned out to be real. The weight of the decision held Alix captive. She had to decide, so she chose to believe in Meredith and her magic.

Alix nodded, gripping her father's hand, barely registering the circle of knights that had formed around them, all holding swords lit by Anastasia's flames. "Do it," she said. "Save him. Father, I'm sorry." Magic. Conflict twisted, churned in Alix's gut. If her father lived, did this change anything? Could it change anything?

"My sweet, Alixandra," he murmured, closing his eyes. "There's nothing to .... be sorry..." His eyelids fluttered.

Meredith moved her hands over the gaping wound in his neck. The red light of her magic sank into his skin, slowing the continuous leak of blood dripping down his neck. Sweat dappled her forehead as she strained to work on the wounds. "General, how have you stayed standing?" Meredith's magic jumped like lightning across General Xander's body, exposing the places the unnatural strength of the Hollows had torn his armor to shreds. "There's too many... I don't..."

Alix's heart thundered, blocking out every other sound. He had to live. "Daddy, please." Alix squeezed his hand. "Stay. Open your eyes. Stay awake. You can do this, Meredith. You have to do this." Her words rushed out in an angry sob.

"I love you," he said. "I would die a hundred times to save you."

"No, Daddy." Alix pulled his hand to her face, pressing his cold skin against her cheek. "Mere."

"I can't. Alix. My magic. Even with the wellspring so close, I'm using everything I have. If we had another healer, maybe, but I just... I'm not enough." Meredith clenched her fists.

"Then tell me what to do. I'm Silvid, aren't I? Tell me. Use me," Alix demanded, still clinging to her father's hand.

"Alix... I don't think." Meredith stared at her with a tight frown, though her magic still danced along the general's body. She was still trying, despite the way her body trembled from the effort.

Alix took a deep breath. She'd felt it the day the Academy uncovered the wellspring. Magic. It had come in a rush. Exhilarating. Terrifying. Even now, she could feel it screaming for release under her skin. "Use me," she said again. The red rush of magic jolted out of Alix and pooled around them like a fog.

Meredith gasped, her own magic faltering for a moment. She slid her hand through the air, dragging Alix's magic into a tight ball that danced between her fingertips. "This might not work," Meredith warned, even as she began weaving the red light in the air to direct it into the general's open wounds.

"Just do something!" Alix's muscles tightened painfully as she doubled over her father's body. She'd never released it before, never let the magic get the better of her. Now that she'd opened the gates, it flooded from her. Neon magic hung in the air, blinding her. Meredith worked silently beside her, harnessing the energy Alix offered.

Time passed. Mere minutes felt like hours. When the red light finally cleared, Alix found that she and Meredith were alone, huddled over her father. The other knights scattered across the desert plateau, tending to the injured and gathering the bodies of their fallen. The Hollows were gone and the night, which had once wrapped around them with bloodlust on the wind, now succumbed to the first rays of sunrise.

Alix forced herself to look at her father. The tear at his throat had become a gnarled scar. All of his injuries were smoothed over, yet his eyes were closed. She held her breath and brought her shaking fingers beneath his nose. Relief washed over her as she felt the soft rush of his breath. He was alive. Her father lived.

Alix sat back in the sand. "Mere. You did it," she said, looking over at her mate, who knelt beside her.

Meredith's skin was pale and sweat slid down her face, soaking into the collar of the tunic beneath her armor. "We did it," she said. Her voice shook. Her dark eyes were ringed in bright red, the same color as the Hollow's eyes. The sight unsettled her, but Alix wouldn't focus on that or her now conflicting feelings about magic. Their mate bond warmed in Alix's chest as their mutual relief and joy ran back and forth across the bond's thread. Alix felt the shift before she saw it. Confusion, then fear, replaced the relief in the bond thread.

Meredith's head tilted and her eyes slid shut as she pitched forward. Alix yelped as she scrambled towards Meredith, catching her before her head could hit the ground. Meredith's body relaxed in Alix's arms, growing limp as her breath evened out. She'd fainted again. Alix held Meredith against her chest, squeezing her as tight as she dared.

Footsteps thundered across the sandstone, drawing Alix's attention. Anastasia, covered in blood and bruises, led a group of knights to their side. "Let's get them down to Haven," Anastasia ordered. The knights were quick to obey, loading the general onto a stretcher. When they reached for Meredith, Alix jerked away.

"I'll carry her," she said.

Anastasia smiled. "Let me help you."

The sun peeked above the horizon, sending light scattering and shimmering across the distant sands. Its rays seared Alix's skin, and she nodded. The quicker they could get out of the growing heat, the better. With Anastasia's help, Alix stood with Meredith in her arms. The knights, with the general held aloft between them, followed Anastasia and Alix to the wagon that had brought the Academy's explosives.

The queen's plan had utterly failed. Her father nearly died. At least a dozen knights had fallen to the Hollows. Meredith and Alix both had actually used magic. Things were changing. Apprehension sank its claws into her heart. The Hollows were to blame. All of this suffering was their fault.

Holding Meredith tight in her lap, Alix rode in the wagon with her sleeping father and the girl who had protected them when he'd nearly died. Alix had every intention of seeing this fight to the end, which now seemed to mean she would spend a lot more time in Haven with Anastasia and the human knights. Together, they would destroy the Hollows, no matter what it took.

CHAPTER 21

Anastasia

Nearly a week had passed since the battle in the desert. Life continued to change. Sightings of the Hollows only grew with each day. Then, the queen's orders came—Alix would replace the Haven general who had fallen. She and Meredith were now more permanent residents of Haven. Anastasia was glad they would both be staying, especially since their help would be crucial to dealing with the Hollows, but the circumstances were heartbreaking. So many had died that day, and so many more would die before the Hollow War, as the queen was now calling it, would be over.

Anastasia stood in the sanctuary of the Western Temple. Meredith and Alix stood beside her, while General Xander sat in a chair to the right of Alix, clutching a cane in his hand. The sanctuary had once been empty — a strange leftover place of worship from ancient times, but now it was a graveyard.

Fourteen glass coffins lined the front of the room and hundreds of people from Haven stood in silence. Her father,

Commander Creon, leader of Haven, stood alongside the empty coffins.

"Today, we have lost fourteen warriors who were well-loved by the people of Haven." His voice boomed, bouncing against the stone floors and walls, which glowed with the sacred flame. The fire, which had been brought to life by the head mage of Haven's Mage Tower, moved like honey through the crevices of the temple.

The crowd waited, hanging on his words. Despite the warmth and familiarity of the flame, grief and fear held Anastasia captive. She'd barely survived that fight herself. If she hadn't been able to pull magic from the wellspring using the sigil that Shiloh taught her, the deaths would have been far greater. Truthfully, if the sun hadn't risen, they might have all died, anyway.

A slow, mournful song rose from the hallway beyond the sanctuary. The song drew closer, until a line of knights broke into the room, carrying the dead, who were dressed in unmarred Haven regalia—leather and chainmail painted with the gold and red emblem of Haven. As Creon announced the name of each warrior, the knights lowered the dead into their coffins.

"Marcus Cresthallow," Creon said, pausing as the familiar body was lowered into the coffin. He'd been one of her father's closest knights, possibly even one of his friends, but Anastasia didn't let herself look long. She didn't want to think about the people she'd lost or the ones she was sure to lose soon.

"Damien Shaw." The list of names continued on. "Sarah Moush. Latrish Bearn. Dominic Ogan." Anastasia squeezed her eyes shut, letting the names hit her ears, as she vowed to not forget their sacrifice. She would protect Haven. Anastasia would give everything to keep her people safe.

She glanced at the women beside her. Alix stood with her hands on the back of her father's wooden chair. Meredith, with one hand intertwined with Alix's, watched the funeral procession with furrowed brows and tears glimmering in her eyes. Noticing Anastasia's stare, Meredith slid an arm through Anastasia's.

"Thank you," Meredith whispered. "Without you and the knights keeping the Hollows at bay, the general would—"

Anastasia nodded. "You're part of Haven now. Don't thank me. It's my duty."

"Right," she said, glancing back at Alix.

Alix leaned towards Anastasia and Meredith, lowering her voice to a whisper. "Nevertheless, I am in your debt. I will fight by your side until this is over."

"As will I," Meredith said, clinging to Alix's hand. Anastasia could tell how much the battle had scared her. Meredith hadn't left Alix's side since they'd all returned from the desert. But this was just the beginning of the fear and suffering.

The Hollow horde grew each day, though no one knew why. Meredith continued to research and the rest of them continued to train.

Together, the three of them would end the Hollow war. Anastasia didn't know how, only that they would. She was born to protect Haven as the Keeper of Light, but she was glad that now, she didn't have to carry the weight on her own.

***

Thank you for reading! If you enjoyed this story, you might enjoy *The Court of Dreams*, which is set about 25 years after *The Keeper of Light*, and follows Lana, a waitress from Feyville, Florida, who gets caught up in the Hollow war. Familiar characters pop up once Lana gets to the Court of Dreams (Shiloh, Anastasia, Vasileios, Alix, and Meredith).

The Court of Dreams is available for preorder for only 4.9 9$. Order now to get it as soon as it releases! www.books2re ad.com/courtofdreams

Preorder the next book in the series at ajnorabooks. com

The Court of Dreams for 3.99$!

Again, thank you so much for reading. I really appreciate your support. As an indie author, your support means that I can continue writing. My lifelong dream has always been to be a full-time author. Buying my books, reviewing this book, and telling your friends about my book helps me achieve my dream, so thank you (from me and my orange gremlin, Kiwi!)

About the Author

A.J. Nora is a queer author from the deep south, who writes epic fantasy with romance. She loves swords and magic, fated mates, and faerie royalty. She became obsessed with faeries after reading the Fae Fever series when she was in high school. Ever since then, she's been writing down her daydreams, hoping to share them with the world.

If you'd like to come along on her indie author journey, follow A.J. on social media:

Facebook : https://m.facebook.com/61561948896462/

Instagram: https://www.instagram.com/ajnorabooks/

TikTok: https://www.tiktok.com/@ajnorabooks

Bluesky: https://bsky.app/profile/ajnorabooks.bsky.social

Tumblr: https://www.tumblr.com/ajnorabooks

www.ingramcontent.com/pod-product-compliance
Lightning Source LLC
Chambersburg PA
CBHW031051310726

48969CB00007B/2217